L&D The Chronicles of Life and Death.

This Book is devoted to everyone that always said I could, to my Drill Sergeants who showed me that I could, and to one very special person that always knew I could.

I0532584

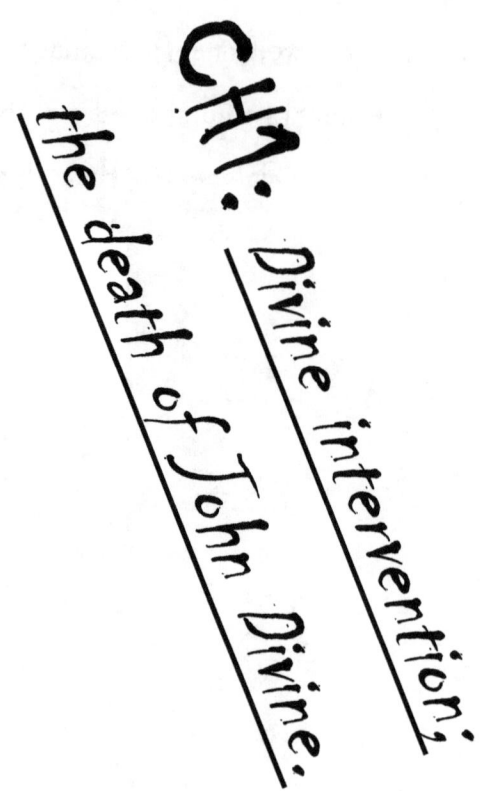

CH1: Divine intervention; the death of John Divine.

March 11 2003: 10:45pm

On a dimly lit street, while walking home from my job at "The pizza shack" my life changed forever. Or maybe I should say my fate changed. I saw what I thought was a robbery in progress. I hid behind some bushes and listened, learning more than I could comprehend at the time.

There was a towering figure masked by shadows and a small man, no taller than 5ft, with an odd smile that would warm the coldest of hearts and an honest demeanor to match. In a deep soul crushing voice the shadowed figure bellowed to the small man.

"Mr. Divine, I have come for your immortal soul. Please save us both some trouble and accept your fate with dignity!"

"While I can appreciate how you angels have such magnificent manners, I am afraid your current offer does not meet my requirements at this time.   Your purpose may be to keep the balance of life and death, however mine is a little more important at the moment. I need to save Mr. Mittens! "

The peculiar little man spoke in calm, yet cheerfully determined manner. Despite the hostility he was shown by the foreboding figure before him.

At once the scene changed from that of a talk, as a hand that looked more like a fist full of daggers, plunged through the smiling man's chest. He keeled over, apparently dead. His last words pulling me out into his world: "Hey you in the bushes...s-save M-Mr. Mittens!"

At once my heart started pounding, like an elephant in a washing machine. What was this guy's game? Why did he have to drag me into this? Why is he so obsessed with a cat?! And is my own life now in danger from this murderous "angel"? One of my questions was quickly answered after I started to regain my composure.

Sitting there dumbfounded, behind the bushes, the angel turned to me and said something I thought I would never forget.

"Forget what you saw, forget what you heard. It is not yet your time Mr. Leon, But if you pursue his cause it could change that fate!" And with that he vanished. No puff of smoke, or weird trick of the eye, without so much as blinking, he just disappeared. He was gone.

I was left in utter shock at the events that just unfolded, staring at Mr. Divine's seemingly lifeless body. Thousands of thoughts rushed through my mind. Did I just witness a murder? What should I tell the police?

"An angel stuck his hand through him and then disappeared?"

No, I would be called a fool. Or worse, I would be charged with his murder. Shit!   But as I was pondering this; I realized his body was no longer there. Was I going crazy or? No, I knew what I saw, despite having to reassure myself that it had been there.   This must be explainable, somehow. I knew there had to be a reason for all of this.

After the shock wore off, I realized two hours had passed. It was now approaching 1:00 am, I needed to get home. I needed to sleep, but most of all I needed some answers. I walked the rest of the way home, everything else seemed normal but I still jumped at the sound of every passing car, or sound in the distance. I felt paranoid, like someone with arachnophobia passing through a spider museum.

I arrived home at 1:18 am; I quickly shut and locked my door, lest an unseen intruder enter without my knowledge. Reassuring myself as though it could actually help against something like that angel.

So there I sat waiting for a kettle to boil, so I could make some tea to calm down. And a loud knock nearly made me jump out of my already pale skin. I secretly hoped whoever, or whatever it was would go away. Come back tomorrow...or never. But I was met with no such luck. Another couple of loud raps on my door told me I had to do something. Should I run? It was most likely either the cops or that "Angel"; neither of these scenarios seemed favorable to me at the time.

Reluctantly, I headed toward the door, peered out the peephole and nearly fainted. It was the strange little man smiling his contagious grin, and standing on my porch, seemingly unharmed, pounding away on my door. I quickly opened the door and demanded to know exactly what was going on!

"Mr. Leon, while I appreciate your impeccable friendliness as a host, I am afraid I need not take you up on your offer of tea and merely have a request to make."

He said in his seemingly usual pleasant tone. Was he even listening to me? Once more, I demanded to know what was going on!

"Like I said Mr. Leon, despite your wonderfully fulfilling hospitality, I have a favor to ask of you."

His tone, while still friendly, seemed much more compelling and serious this time.

"So how about helping a new friend?"

His smile returning as he spoke.

CH2: Save Mr. Mittens!
And yes, I am dead!

L&D The Chronicles of Life and Death.

"Well friend my time here is short, so please take this book, I wrote down where they are keeping Mr. Mittens on the inside cover..."

Now hold on just a minute, I interrupted.   For one, how are you even alive?!   And for two, why can't you save Mr. Mittens? His response confused me even more, making me wish I had just kept my mouth shut.

"My friend, I am not alive. I am sure you saw me die, earlier? With the hand? Yes. Quite dead. That's also why I can't save Mr. Mittens. But it looks like my time is up. Good Lu-"

And then just as mysteriously as the angel, he was gone.

The unsettling feeling that perhaps I was now the lone person who could save Mr. Mittens was setting in. And why was I even so worried about this Mr. Mittens?

Was a now dead, or sort of dead, possibly un-dead? Man's cat such a big deal? Besides, knowing what that angel had said I should just forget all this, and live my life.

I mean really what a great life I lived. Alone, no girlfriend, dead end job, barely able to pay my bills... This was a risk, but something in me just snapped, and I was feeling compelled to save this strange undeterminably dead (or possibly alive?) man's cat. Maybe my fate was to be a nobody my whole life, forgotten by all when I died, and to be lonely forever. And maybe, just maybe, this was a chance to change that fate!

So it was settled, I decided to save Mr. Mittens! I mean why not? I do have the weekends off. But now I was met with the hardest question; where to begin? Ah! The book! I picked up the book the little man, who's status of life I currently was unsure of, had left for me. It was a rather old and ratty looking book. A dark rich red, with silver wording where it had not worn off, and silver gild pages. I tried to make out the title of the book, from where the letters where not worn completely away. "The chronicles of life and death" Perhaps a fitting name for such a strange book.

I began flipping thru the book, quickly realizing it wasn't just beat up, and every other page in the book was missing. Beyond that, reading the book was just grizzly. The foreword read: "For those who value the life of one, over the many. For the curious of the macabre, for those in a desperate situation who don't care the cost, this book will grant you an immortal soul; if you pay the price. Consider yourself warned."

Flipping through the book, every page seemed to have a different method to become immortal.   Towards the middle of the book, titled: "100 to 1", it read:

"The way of the crooked king, the tyrant who refuses to die. To use this method you must eat the heart of 100 men, and then stab yourself with a frozen dagger, thru your own heart.   Your soul will remain frozen in time, as you are now, as you will remain. To kill the crooked king, read the next page."

The only thing worse than this inhuman method, was the detailed drawings that were illustrating the method. I will save you the gruesome description, but the next page was missing anyway. The whole book seemed to be this way.   Having read enough, I decided to quite reading and flip back to the front cover.

Written, in a very nice cursive script, was simply: "31st & bloom St."

So somewhere, downtown at 31st & bloom, Mr. Mittens was being held captive.

Now I just needed to make a plan.

CH3: The Purr-fect plan.

L&D The Chronicles of Life and Death.

Part 1: Reconnoiter:

The following day I decided to see exactly what I was up against. So I loaded up a cooler with sandwiches and soda, grabbed my binoculars, climbed in my pickup, and was on my way. Arriving around noon, I parked in a gravel lot with a decent view of the intersection and then I started watching to see what I could find out. At the intersection there were 3 empty corner shops and a pet store. At this point, determination wringing in my ears, I was convinced something fishy must be going on at the pet store. (*No pun intended*) However after 3 hours, 2 tuna sandwiches, and 6 sodas, it was rapidly becoming evident that this was just a pet store. Was it really just two crazy old men arguing over a cat that I had seen? Had someone been killed (sort of anyway) over a Cat? *No*, my gut told me there must be more to this crazy story.

L&D The Chronicles of Life and Death.

My gut was also telling me I needed a bathroom, and having already scouted the area, home sounded like the best bet.

Part 2: Action!

After a good night's sleep, hearty breakfast, and a few cups of coffee, I decided that today I would go to the pet store and try to locate Mr. Mittens.

Arriving at the pet store around 11am, I decided just to play it by ear. I simply decided to walk into the pet store. The shelves were lined with all sorts of animals, some perhaps better pets than others. Walking toward the back of the store it soon became clear that despite a wide and very exotic variety of pets, there were no cats to be found anywhere in the store. There were however a fine variety of fish. So yes, there was something fishy about the store.

 I began to see the humor in the whole situation, what was I thinking?   Doing all this over the crazy babbling of some crazy guy, maybe I even imagined all of it? That would make the most sense.

 I decided to just leave; try and forget this whole thing. I mean what harm could it have right?

CH4: Friend or foe? How I wish I could know.

Right as I opened the door of the pet store to leave, I was met with a very unpleasant surprise. The large cloaked figure, so kindly referred to as an "Angel", was standing there. I think he was waiting for me.

He seemed to be even taller this time. I was at a loss for words, the only thing I would've have been more surprised by would be a dog on the roof tap dancing and singing a good old jig. The next 5 minutes seemed like 5 hours as we both stared at each other not a saying a word, until suddenly, that same crushing voice boomed out:

"Mr. Leon, you disappoint me. Do you value your life so little that you are ready to risk it for a cause you don't even comprehend? If that is truly the case, then come to the Sauldaday crypt tomorrow night. I will give you the answers you seem to so desperately want.

Until then, take and wear this cross pendant. It's called a soul stone. They are only bestowed by an angel; this stone cross will protect your soul from all divine beings. Do not lose it Mr. Leon! "

Then he disappeared again. I wasn't sure what to make of this recent turn of events. Just the other day I had feared this angel as a murderous creature, and now he was offering me the answers I wanted. And he gave me a nice fashion statement. Couldn't be that bad right? Well, the main problem? I had to work tomorrow night. Bummer.

Getting up for work the next day seemed harder than usual, this last week had really taken a toll on me, I just felt completely drained. It was also turning out to be a rather bad day. I tripped and fell on my face, found out my milk was spoiled (had to eat dry cereal), and my toaster caught on fire. If you think about it, really, whose toaster catches on fire? Not the start of a million dollar day. Hell, not the start of a $5 day for that matter.

I did my best to pull myself together, I put on my uniform and decided to start heading toward work. The walk seemed longer than usual. Recent events were still fresh in my mind, so much so that I couldn't seem to focus. I ran into 3 people, nearly knocking them over. And I tripped on the curb, face first, leaving a nice gash across my face. The distraction of my own thoughts seemed to have me in my own world.

Arriving at work just a few minutes early, I was thankfully at least in uniform. To my dismay however, my boss didn't agree. He claimed that I was late. Even after arguing that the clocks at pizza shack haven't even been reset since daylight savings, it was no use. And to make matters worse, I was called into the little joke of an office we had for the dreaded "Let's talk". Nobody in the history of mankind has retained gainful employment after hearing these words; not around these parts anyway.

"Even though you are a seemingly model employee, you show up late, and looking like death, I am afraid you have just made my decision much easier. You can finish up the week if you want, but next week I expect you to be gone"

Apparently it was time to downsize the crew, and I had just walked into drawing the short straw. No amount of groveling would change his mind; I tried until finally being asked to leave the building. More like forcefully escorted by the police after trying to change his mind by way of screaming; in hindsight maybe not the best strategy, but at the time it felt great. Got all of that pent up aggression out. Well, I guess tonight was free after all.

With nothing else to do the rest of the day, I stopped by "Javax", the local coffee shop. The ever lovely Lola was making my coffee. As I fantasized about the future we would have someday, if I ever could muster up the nerve to ask her out on a date that is, (I have tried and failed so many times after losing my nerve.) I was suddenly snapped back to my senses.

"Mr. Leon, Mr. LEON!"

Oh! My apologies, how much will that be? Right same as always, $3.50.....Say, Lola.....

"Yes? What is it?"

"Would you like to go to dinner next week?"

(I couldn't believe it; I was actually asking her, the girl I so secretly longed for, on a date! Wait I was doing what?! Oh man your right, this was a terrible idea. Why didn't you say something?! Yes you, the reader! You're like god right now. By the way, you're a terribly mean and awful god; setting me up for failure. I hate you now; I don't believe in you anymore! I am not going to talk to you anymore.)

"Sorry I have a boyfriend.   Anything else I can do for you Mr. Leon?"

"No, thank you though."

Rejection, just as I had feared so many times before. Oh well just another disappointment to add to my week.

CH5: Dante, the angel of death.

The rest of the day past uneventfully, soon enough the sun was setting and I was making my way to the Sauldaday crypt. But thoughts were starting to creep into my mind, should I really be going there alone? After all, it could be a trap. Over all the risk seemed worthwhile to finally start getting some answers.

Upon arrival at the crypt, a sense of unease was seriously setting in. Against my better judgment I decided to shake it off and keep going. Sure enough sitting on the floor in the crypt was the angel I had now come to know as "Shit, it's that guy again". But his demeanor seemed more inviting than it had previously, at least to the point where I didn't feel as though he was about to rip my throat out. Upon noticing my arrival he quickly rose and bellowed out in his ever intimidating voice:

"Leonardo Otis Leon I am pleased you decided to hear me out. Despite recent events I and the organization I represent are not interested in pointless killing. The man you witnessed me kill was actually part of a very dangerous group. They call themselves the masterminds. But perhaps it would be better if I start from the beginning.

As long as man has existed he has fought against time, trying to make a mark in this world with his insignificant life. Death is ever looming over his soul, waiting for his time to be up. As soon as it is, death is charged with the job of collecting his soul. Not out of spite, but to maintain balance and order. After all everyone must have a beginning, middle, and end.

The main problem started about 500 years ago. A group of brilliant men, masterminds in their own respect, faced death. It was there time to die but they refused to go, instead, they tricked death. They had somehow crafted a spell, out of the darkest of dark magic, and cast an incantation on death. So long as he could see them, they would forever remain out of reach.

   Having achieved this victory over death the masterminds failed to remain content for long.   They chose to delve even deeper in to the world of dark sorcery to find ways that others could cheat death, for death is never fooled the same way twice. They ended up writing a book called: "The Chronicles of Life and death." In it, they detailed every new way they found to become immortal, and the weakness of each new mastermind.

   Once death can no longer grip you, your soul becomes immortal, no one can collect it. It bypassed

the natural order; the system that was put into place
long ago. The problem with this is that it throws the
world into chaos. What if Hitler had never died? What
horrid monstrosities, such as famine, drought, and
disease would arise from such overpopulation? The
world needs death to retain plausible population levels
to maintain a decent quality of life; the resources
present are limited.

 The angels in charge of maintaining balance and order
decided to have an emergency council. After much
investigation, we learned of the book they had written
and we spent hundreds of years tracking it down.
However, as soon as they realized we knew about it
they removed all the pages detailing their weaknesses
and hid them. However, even without those pages they
continued passing the book around the world, recruiting
more souls for the evil cause they had created. Using

horrendous acts of the dark art and causing massive havoc across the world, their numbers grow every year.

Knowing we couldn't claim their souls, a new strategy was used. Capture them and lock them away, in a prison of sorts, made specifically for these new immortals. It was called "The stone stronghold". But, they fought back with an ever increasing arsenal of hex, spell, and dark weapons they had developed to work against us. Angels are immortal after all; we can die, just not of age. We were created as light in the darkness, and the darkness can reclaim us. We have no souls to anchor us in this plain of existence. Purpose alone is what anchors us here. Our souls are collected when we are created."

"And now I am sure you are wondering what this has to do with you, is that correct Mr. Leon?"

He asked, lowering his hood so I could see his face clearly for the first time. I nodded yes; as I took in the revelation of his almost human appearance. His face was young, like someone in their 20's, with a single horrific scar around his left eye in the shape of a pentagram with 3 uneven circles around it and a strike vertically thru the center, His left eye seemed to be sealed shut from this scar. His dark hair had almost a metallic shimmer to it. His right eye was a mix of green and blue, in a "Ying-Yang" pattern.

"Well Mr. Leon, you are the next target. They mean to make you immortal using that book, of which I am sure he has already given to you. So, now you must make a choice. Will you choose to help us? Or will you choose your own selfish desires over the lives of so many innocent people?"

I have thumbed through that book, and can tell you I would never use any of those atrocities. But I still don't understand what I could possibly do to help you. I'm not some divine being like you are, I am just a regular person; and if you can't kill these Masterminds how exactly is it you killed John Divine?! I harked back at him.

"Mr. Leon, angels possess the equivalent of the dark magic used by them, however it is fueled by the very light of our being, and we use it to channel the natural energy around us. Where their powers are fueled from the blackened souls they possess.

The mark over my left eye allows me a sort of second sight. To overcome the original incantation used against me, I had to make it where I could not see them at all. All I have to do is place a copy of this marking on someone and it allows me to track where they are. I collect their soul without ever "seeing them". However aside from the original few, this method does not work on anymore, the newer batches of immortals are far harder to kill. Mr. Mittens and John divine were the last of the originals, both of whom I have dispatched to the next plain of existence."

"But why ME!? You can have that book; I don't need or want it! I can give it to you tonight if you want! I just want to be done with this; I don't want to end up dead..."

"Mr. Leon, only you can safeguard the book right now... if you give it to us they will just kill you, and kill whichever of us has the book to get it back. They want you Leonardo, you have nobody to miss you, no one to ask why you do not age, and you have potential.

So long as you keep the book for them, play along, and wear that stone I have given you, you should be safe."

"SHOULD BE??"

He said something under his breath, and gave me a push, nearly knocking me over. Just as I was about to ask him what exactly that was about he began violently coughing, keeled over, and a bright luminous liquid began running from his nose and mouth, bright enough to be light itself. I caught him as he fell, but his moment of weakness did not seem to pass. Could this have been his own divine blood that he was coughing up?

"I'm afraid I must go now Leonardo. I am afraid I have fulfilled my purpose here...there will be a new angel of death soon. This is goodbye Leonardo, and thank you for restoring my hope...of the existence of a pure soul. I am glad I spared your soul when that vehicle crashed all those years ago... I saw potential in its pureness and broke divine law to give you a chance to live. I have watched you from the shadows for all of these years to make sure I had not made a mistake, I saw you cry, saw you love, and saw you live. I am proud of the man you have become Leonardo."

As I listened to his words I realized that this whole time he must have been what had protected me in the crash that killed everyone else in my family. Thinking back, I remembered seeing him. He was walking away from the crash as I woke up. He had looked over his shoulder and said: Don't be afraid to live your life young one.

How could I have forgotten that metallic hair? All of these fleeting glimpses rushed back to memory of close calls I had. Thinking about it, he must have been there for all of them. I now remembered seeing him so many times but had never connecting the dots.

He just smiled, realizing I had finally remembered him, and said:

"My name was Dante, the angel of death. And now..."

But he stopped speaking mid-sentence, as his eyes became cold and distant I knew exactly what had happened. He started disappearing, not like before, but this time it was different, it was slower than before; As if the light that gave form to his very being was fading into the shadows. It was like watching a dying star. I held him until there was nothing left but his cloak. Sitting there alone in the crypt holding his cloak, I couldn't help but feel I had lost a lifelong friend. Such

L&D The Chronicles of Life and Death.

was my life; everyone I cared for seemed to die or disappear.

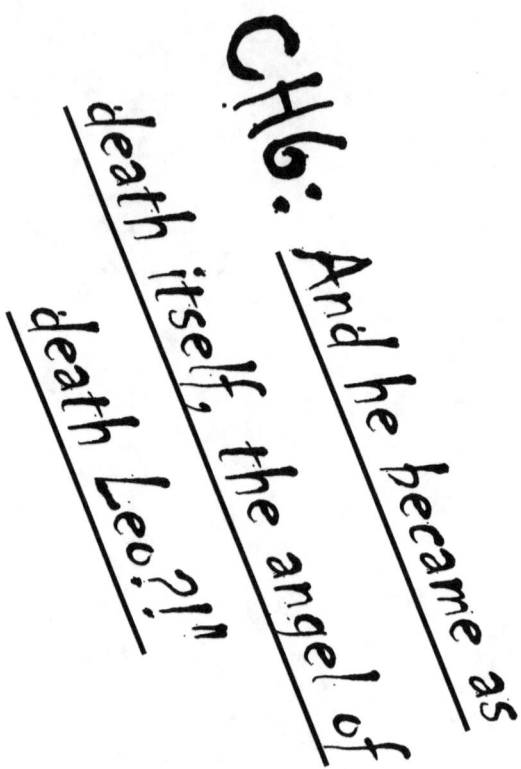

CH6: And he became as death itself, the angel of death Leo?!"

I spent that entire night sitting in the crypt. I was trying to figure out what to do next. Upon the revelation that perhaps my fate was involved in all of this from the start. But what do I do now? The only ones I knew of were all dead. At some point during the night I fell asleep.

I awoke to a mellow whisper of a lovely girl's voice.

"These are words of Dante of the seven, maybe you should try them?"

Then she giggled and said:

"Banish thy evil, banish thy fear live your life for I am here! Let darkness fade to light, as any unjust by divine law fear my might! Of the seven angels I am the end. The hour of death draws near, stand your ground or run in fear, the angel of death Dante is here!"

I stood up, quickly surveying the crypt, no one was there. Then the previous night's events started to flood back into my mind it was overwhelming but somewhere deep down I knew morning his death would do nothing for me right now, so I pulled myself together and decided to try it. What harm could it do?

"Banish thy evil, banish thy fear, live your life for I am here! Let the darkness fade to.....hmmm I forgot the rest.   Something something Dante is here!"

As I had suspected nothing of significance happened; unless you include a sneeze; I did feel a sudden urge to sneeze.

"You're silly! Maybe you should make up your own incantation Mr. new angel of death."

That same voice, I turned around quickly to see a small hooded figure, this one was only 5 ft. tall, with long pink hair barely hidden behind her hood and the sweet voice I had previously heard.

"What is your name anyway new angel of death? Dante said he found someone special, but I didn't realize he meant his replacement. I wouldn't have been late if I knew that! And why are you wearing those silly things instead of your cloak? Are you asking to get killed? And where is your halo? Don't tell me you were alive!? That's just cruel. But then again, Dante really never respected those kinds of boundaries."

"My name is Leonardo, and what do you mean his replacement? I am a human! Not some angel!"

"Ha-ha guess again sucker!"

She snickered at me trying to stifle a full on laughing spell at my expense. Clearly see was seeing some humor in this whole misunderstanding.

"Dante always did like to break the rules, always using incantations, and that one time. Can you believe he spared a child's soul, just on a whim? Lost his halo and his wings for that one! Said something about the child being special. Should've just let the brat die if you ask me!"

"That brat was me!"

I angrily snarled at her as indignant rage began to cloud my mind. Her disrespect of the one person who watched over me from the shadows, and cared when I thought I had nobody was pushing my anger button; hard.

"Oh...I see...please forgive my rudeness then. Clearly he didn't tell you about his intentions then, did he? You poor thing..."

"I'm sorry but exactly who are you, and why do you keep calling me an angel?"

I snapped, interrupting her. I was tired of just getting laughed at and having no earthly idea what the hell was going on.

"Hahaha, ok ya impatient brat, I'm Runa 6, of the seven angels. I am called the angel of life. Where Dante took life, I bestow it."

"THEN BRING DANTE BACK YOU HAG!"

I yelled, my anger completely overtaking me, and my voice getting much deeper than normal. I was momentarily taken aback by my abrupt change in tone, I felt like someone else had spoken in my place.

"Look kid, I will give you the benefit of the doubt here, but be careful who you lose your cool around. You are an angel now whether you like it or not. And not all angels would be this understanding. I know you've been through a lot, but just look at your own reflection kid. You aren't human anymore! "

I rushed over to the polished marble wall and saw, to my horror, my formerly black hair now had a metallic tinge, and my right eye had a green and blue swirl in a Ying-Yang pattern. My left eye had a green pentagram over my formerly all blue eye. What happened to me!? I started freaking out. This must be from that stone cross! But it was gone. Instead I had what looked to be a grey tattoo where it had been. I frantically scratched at it, trying to get it off, but nothing happened. Runa came over to try and calm me down.

"Look Leonardo...no that won't do, how about Leo? That work for you?"

I nodded yes; her voice seemed to calm me down, like a mother cooing her child.

"You need to relax. It's not that bad, right? I will teach you about being an angel of seven, and everything will be ok. The first thing you need to know is that the cloak you have is called a divine cloak, it cannot be ripped, torn, or burned, and will help protect you, so put it on. Next thing is now that you're a divine being you won't ever die of old age. But you can still die if you're not careful.

The masterminds have it out to kill you just like they tried to with Dante. Though all seven of us were once charged with separate jobs, because of the Masterminds, I am also a working angel of death, to help you. The Ring council has put lesser divine being in charge of my original job.

You and I are now charged with restoring the balance of life and death. You also don't have a halo, which could be a problem, so I will go meet with the ring council to see what I can do about that. Wait for me here alright?"

I nodded yes, as she disappeared in a Bright flash. I really needed to learn how to do that.

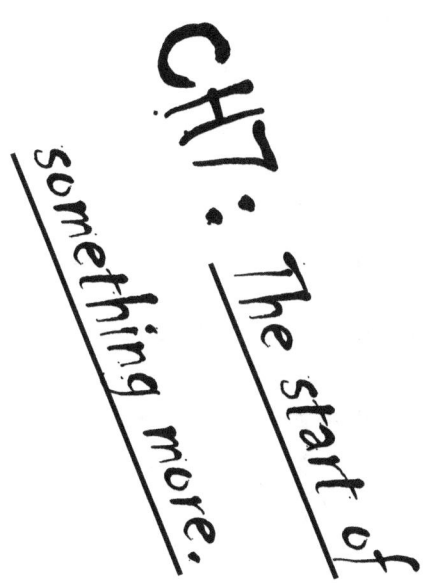

CH7: The start of something more.

After Runa left, I took the chance to leave undetected. I quickly put on the cloak and fastened my hood. I was soon moving far away from the crypt. Moving through the city streets I took notice how nobody seemed to notice me. Unless I spoke to them they didn't seem to see me at all. As soon as I spoke to them no, as soon as I made eye contact with them, they seemed to be able to see me.

I just kept my head down and walked through town. I was not sure where to go yet so I headed toward the pet store where I had actually met Dante. To my surprise it was gone. All that was left was a vacant shop front. Something fishy was going on here. As I peered through the window a voice behind me prompted my attention.

"Bravo Mr. Leon, guessing from the cloths you have killed Dante, am I correct? But I must ask, have you decided to become an angel?"

He spoke in the voice of a gentleman from the 40's; I turned around and saw that he also dressed the part.

"I didn't have a choice in the matter!   And your bunch killed Dante, not me!"

"I see, so Mr. Mittens was able to succeed before his end, placing a delayed hex incantation to kill Dante. Very good news this is then. Well Mr. Leon I am not sure what to do with you now, being an angel and all. How about you just hold on to that book for now? We never actually intended to recruit you, but we could use your assistance, will you help us? "

He had the same smile as John divine, and reached out an open hand as he asked.

"Why would you think I would want to help any of you with anything?!"

"Because my dear boy, there are two sides to every story and I was hoping you would have the patience to hear our side before you so harshly judge us. After I am done talking you can even kill me if you would like."

"I am not here to kill you! I don't want to kill anyone!"

I snapped in my now powerful voice.

"Fantastic! Where shall I begin?"

"I'm sure the angels of seven have informed you of our longstanding history. So I will just cover our most current dilemma. Currently the masterminds as a collective entity have ceased to be. Living for so long we have learned to regret our horrible misdeeds. But we have also learned things that deserve to be shared

- 52 -

with all of humanity. Secrets of the world that transcend the possibility technology will ever have. With simple words we are able to do almost anything, on a whim none the less! And we have been working on newer less violent ways to become immortal, they had shown great promise; ways that only affect the one using it. That archaic book you have is a relic of the past, for most of us anyway. There are still a few still claiming the name of mastermind that cling to the old ways, we too are trying to eliminate them, but the angel's current method is just cruel.

Catching one of us, they dismember, remove the tongue, and gouge the eyes out. They are then put into a solid stone cube to remain for the rest of eternity. They call this system of torture a "soul prison.

The angels know how to kill me; I made this bargain with the ring council, to be spared from getting the fate worse than death they refer to as soul prison. I am also refined to this building and had my incant abilities sealed."

He held out his arms, and pointed to the side of his neck. There were double pentagrams over both. He further explained to me that the single pentagram was used to focus the natural energy around you, but with the double pentagram it reverses the focus. If he tried to incant anything, quite simply put, it would blow his arms and head off. He was immortal, but living life as a severed head was un-appealing to him.

I asked him exactly what the point of all this was, what did he need from me?

He smiled, said he was terribly sorry for all this and then with an open palm struck my stomach. While doing so he yelled out what sounded like an incantation.

"Mycanath sythos doriam nobajjagojos!

Clearly an incant of some sort as his head and arms proceeded to blow up. As his head roll around on the floor, missing large chunks of bone and flesh, he simply said: "With that, you are the hope of the-"

In a bright flash Runa appeared, you are in SO MUCH trouble now Soma! You were forbidden to use incants. What have you done? Hope it was worth it, the ring council ordered me to imprison you if you ever broke the agreement. She then held up her finger and blew on it producing a huge flame. It completely engulfed Soma, encircling all of his splattered bits and turned to solid stone.

"Leo he was a terrible man, I hope you didn't listen to anything he said."

She snapped her fingers and the cube started glowing, and then just disappeared.

I really wanted to ask her how they were able to make everything disappear like that, but instead I settled on confronting her about the soul prisons.

"Like about the soul prisons you put these poor people in?!"

"Oh Leo, don't you get it yet? These people are murderers, they are not owed anything, and we have to do all that to ensure they can no longer incant and harm anyone."

"Then what about soma? What did he do that was so horrible?"

"Soma was the mastermind of ice, and very dangerous. He killed a lot on innocent people. That's all you need to worry about right now. Come on Leo; let's get back to the crypt there still some stuff I need to teach you about being an angel. But we are now running late thanks to your little field trip, guess we will have to fly"

At which point she grabbed my shoulder and starting yelling very loudly directly into my ear. I did not appreciate it either.

"Forever red, roses of blood, your light I shall bring, life to everything. I am Runa6 of the 7, bringer of life!"

And in an instant it felt as if I was being drug through deep pit of gravel. Time and space was twisting around us, everything was a blur, then in what sounded like a banshee scream we snapped into place at the crypt.

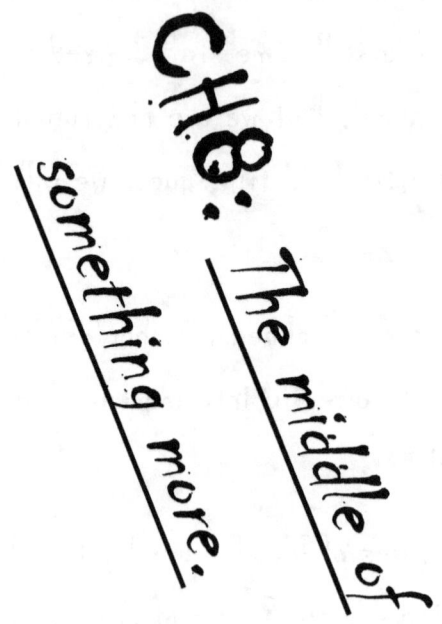

CH8: The middle of something more.

"What did you just do Runa?"

   I asked in disbelief, not entirely sure if I was amazed or horrified, before I threw up all over the crypt floor."

"It's Runa6! And divine beings travel by Wingwave. Well, I guess that would make much sense either, let me explain. You have a pass phrase that activates a mark you are given. The mark then concentrates the natural energy around you at the right frequencies and you get swept to the last location you used it from. Kind of a pain if you use it to get out of somewhere you don't want to be, you'll end up back there next time you use it. You should be able to use it soon, I convinced the ring council to grant you a halo and wings. The first time you use it you will end up back in the crypt"

"Wait so I am going to have wings and a ring of light over my head? Am I allowed to refuse? I would really would prefer to look somewhat normal, no offense."

"Wow you weren't a winner in the thinking game were ya Leo? I just told you what the wings are. It's just a mark on your back in the shape of a wing that concentrates the energy around you at a specific wavelength and shifts you to the last location used. You just have to figure out what you want to say to activate it, and after you get your wing mark the first things you say will be your pass phrase. Depending on how strong your angelic abilities manifest it could be as short as 5 words like the supreme ring leaders, or as long as 30, so be careful to remember what you say. You were alive before becoming an angel so you will probably have a pretty long one. The halo is just a ring mark on the back of your neck that enables you to communicate with other angels by pressing it. Kind of like a radio. "

"Wow that's actually kind of cool, so how do I get these marks? Is it like a tattoo?"

"Not quite Leo, we have to use these, issued by the ring council."

She held up two pieces of paper with weird symbols on them and began to apologize, saying it would be rather unpleasant. She then yelled an incant.

"Roa dusso hijjia myamia!"

The papers flew up in the air and burst into flame. The flames took the form of snakes and flew toward me. Upon impacting my skin my whole body started burning, it felt like I was being burned alive. After the crippling pain had subsided fifteen minutes later, Runa again warned me to remember everything I say next, and to make sure it wasn't something I said very often, otherwise I would end up doing a lot of back tracking.

I really wasn't sure what to say at this point, I had been known to forget things. As I was thinking my mind started to wander toward thoughts of soma. What exactly had he done to me? Should I tell Runa? No, I don't know what she would do to me. Just then I was whisked away from my daydream, Runa was impatiently yelling at me to just say something!

"Black orchid wilt to my touch, of the beginning middle and end, I am the end, THE ANGEL OF DEATH LEO! Is that enough Runa?"

"Well, we had better hope so, or you'll feel kind of silly having to ask me if that's enough every time. Let's go outside and we can check."

Outside of the crypt Runa told me to clear my mind before I used the pass phrase, otherwise it might not work at all. She also told me that the greater energy you put into saying it the greater the effect is: If you say it slowly it happens slowly.

"Ok, wish me luck Runa! Black orchid-"

Everything blurred with the familiar sensation of being drug through a gravel parking lot. And in a loud scream and snap I was back inside the crypt. A moment later Runa came running in.

"Leo what have you done?! No one except the supreme ring leader of the angel council has enough angelic power manifested to activate Wingwave in five words...and you just said two. What did Soma do to you?! ANSWER ME LEO!"

"He was trying to use some sort of incant, but it didn't have time to work before he blew up. I feel fine; it didn't do anything to me."

"Leo you don't understand, it must have. To fly with two words is not possible unless you still have a soul. Angels are forbidden to possess a soul. The angelic conversion process purges your soul, replacing it with pure light energy. Leo you need to go, NOW! "

Runa calm down, I am sure there must be some other explanation for it.

She then told me why we were forbidden to have a soul.

"If you have a soul, and it mixes with the light energy, you can end up with power equal to the gods themselves. They have most likely already sent a kill team Leo. If you don't run now, you will die! *RUN YOU IDIOT! GO!*"

Tears falling down her face as she said this to me, I realized perhaps I wasn't the only one who had been deeply affected by Dante's death. I began running; I didn't even know where to go. I heard five screams behind me in the crypt. The kill team must have been there. I then heard what I would never forget: Runa, begging and screaming for mercy, screaming for her life itself. But I couldn't turn back now; I was too much of a coward. I had to just keep running, trying to block the horrendous sounds out. Until finally, in the distant background, I heard one last blood curdling scream.

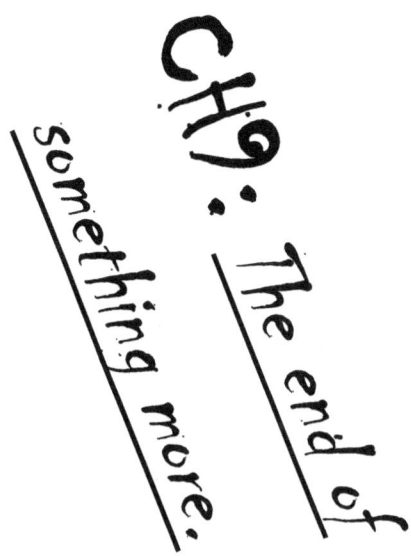

CH9: The end of something more.

Why did it have to be like this? Everyone I began to care about was taken from me. Maybe I really was the angel of death; everything I touch did seem to die. I blamed myself for all of it.

I ran until all I could see around me were trees. I was starting to think I was safe, until, to my horror, I heard five distinct screams in the distance. How had they found me this fast? If they could find me this fast how could I ever escape? No time to think! I started running again. Explosive voices behind me bellowed out.

"Leonard Leon, AKA: The Angel of death Leo, you have been condemned to eternal imprisonment by order of the gods for breaking divine law supreme order 144; possession of a soul by means of dark incant. To be enforced by squad 77 of the ring council immediately. Running will not save you. We will destroy you!"

No matter how fast I ran, or where I went they kept catching up to me. I kept running anyway, finally ending up in the middle of the city, and running through the downtown area looking for some way to lose them. A horrible thought crept into my mind; nobody will even miss me if I die. I had to do something, but no one could even see me unless I made eye contact, or could they? People seemed to be taking notice of me running like a madman. Soma really must have done something after all; but what had he done?

Screams all around me as they snapped into place, I was surrounded. What can I do? What can I do?! Frantically searching for some way out of this mess, Nothing. The kill squad circling inward, I took notice of their distinct appearance; each was wearing a ragged black cloak. They had no face, only a skull, some with large chunks missing. The light of their being seemed to burn like a raging fire from their eyes. Their hands were also skeletal in composition, not a shred of skin in sight.

The leader stepped forward and spoke in a voice that sounded like it was comprised of pure hatred.

"Bahaha, you have been cornered. Now YOU ARE DONE!"

He held up a finger. I knew what was next, soon I would be burned alive, and lord knows what else. Just as he was exhaling, he stopped, exploding into dust. Then I heard what I had missed before, a familiar voice. It was the girl from Javax, Lola?!

"Condusa morasimo forexis demiyoos trigon!!"

Another one exploded into dust. She was holding her right hand up in the air, a glowing triangle with an eye in the center was on her palm. I was incredibly confused as to what was happening, but also incredibly happy that something had stopped that crazy skull guy; I never liked him.

"Kill the target, and anyone that gets in the way!" They turned toward her, still far outnumbering her. She kept firing at them with her incant, but they began dodging it and closing in on her. If I didn't do something she would die, just like Runa. But there was nothing I could do. Why didn't Runa or Dante teach me to incant?

They pinned her against a wall, watching helplessly I couldn't think of anything to do.

"You are the hope! Do something hopeful!!!"

She screamed at me, the desperation in her voice distorting the normal lovely tone she possessed. What hope could I be? There was nothing I could do but watch her die. The anger of my present situation began welling up. Why did everyone have to die? Why? Why?! WHY?! NO MORE! It's me they wanted; I wouldn't let her die too.

Running at them I grabbed all of them in a huge bear hug, struggling to hold everyone.

"BLACK ORCHID!"

Blur, the pain of being drug through gravel, I quickly released them, and before I even snapped into place, I screamed with every bit of my being against the distortion around me.

"B L A C K   O R C H I D!!"

Snap. With a large thud I ended up back with Lola. I keeled over; my whole body felt like I had been beat with a hammer I couldn't even see straight. Everything seemed so distant. Was I dying?

CH10: Dante, Sonia, Lola, and the secret plan of hope.

"Mr. Leon...MR. LEON!"

Was I dead? No, I opened my eyes, I must have blacked out. What happened? Oh god! The kill squad?! I sat up, perhaps a little too quickly, falling right back down. Where was I? I was lying on a bed in an apartment? And smelled... coffee? Lola then walked into the room.

"You gave me quite a scare Mr. Leon; I don't think Dante or Soma would've bet this plan would have worked so well. A two word pass phrase? Amazing! But maybe next time do something like that before I almost get burned alive? Thanks"

She winked as she thanked me, calm as could be.

"Lola, I don't know why you're this calm, but we need to go! The kill squad could be here any minute to Finnish the job."

"Seeing as bits and pieces of them are spread between the city and the crypt I don't think we have to worry about that just yet. Using Wingwave travel to obliterate them was quite brilliant. Something Dante would have done. They were tracking you with your halo. I used a nullifying Trigon to stop that. Dante and soma didn't tell you anything did they?"

She was focusing intently on my reaction, for no apparent reason. It made me feel like a hippopotamus; I think I had a concussion...

"Anything about what? They told me of the history of the Angels and Masterminds. Soma said something about a new problem, and me being the hope, and that jerk used some sort of incant that has apparently got the gods wanting me dead."

"They really didn't tell you anything. There was a legend among the angels, one day a hope would be born, strong enough to kill the gods themselves. The angels have been enslaved by the gods for as long as they have existed. They were created to serve, except some of them secretly resented that. Others happily did their assigned jobs, but for the ones that hated what they had become, they held onto the hope.

See, If the gods needed more angels, they just took more beings from heaven and made them angelic, forever stripping them of their souls and there eternal salvation. One of these angels, Dante, later charged with hunting down the masterminds, quickly learned of the corruption of the gods.

It had been years since they had cared about humanity, they were concerned with making sure no one lived long enough to challenge their control. The angelic legend was dismissed by most everyone as something to console those depressed over their eternal slavery, until that one day, when Dante was sent to collect the souls of a family in a car crash.

He said the soul of a child in the crash was the hope of everything, that the child could someday break the rule of the gods and free the angels. He refused to take that soul, sparing the child and Losing his favor among the gods because of it. Furthermore, since it was him who had been tricked by the masterminds, the gods sentenced him to kill all the original masterminds. What they figured was a death sentence for him given the circumstances. They were, however, wrong.

Dante proved to be tougher than they had expected, killing all the original masterminds. But it was too late; the new masterminds had already spread in numbers far beyond expectation. Searching for a way to become immortal without the monstrosity required by the known methods, they had to recruit increasingly larger numbers, to free humanity. What the gods didn't know was that Dante had helped spread the knowledge of immortality, trying so desperately to find help to overthrow the gods.

But maybe some back story would better illustrate why he turned his back on them. Shortly after Dante died, he was chosen to become an angel. He was furious that he would never get to see his mortal brother Soma in heaven. Somehow, he got his brother the chronicles of life and death, written from the first masterminds. His brother murdered hundreds of people in cold blood, so he could live long enough to help Dante overthrow the gods.

When he was killing John Divine, you just happened to be there, the wrong place at the right time. He told us that at that moment he was sure. You were to one day be the Savior of everything. That you would one day be the one to kill the gods.

You and I are what are left of his rebellion. Everyone else has died for you to have a chance to free us all."

"Why me?! Why couldn't you all fight your own war? I had a life! "

"You're the only one whose soul is capable of it; you weren't doing anything with it. You—"

"BUT IT WAS MY LIFE! I NEVER AGREED TO THIS! ..I'm sorry Lola, but I don't want this, I can't kill gods. I can't even fight. Just leave me alone."

"If you don't do this, then everything Dante worked for, everything we have been fighting for was pointless. Do you realize how greedy you're being? Dante wouldn't have died from his wounds, but he chose to use the last of his angelic power to make sure you kept your soul. He put every last bit of his being into trusting the hope of the world with you! Soma gave his life to use the unsealing incant Dante gave him to free your soul, killing himself."

"Well, then what about Runa? What was her part in this?"

"Oh, well, see, she was kind of just in the wrong place at the wrong time...it would seem..."

"So she just died?! YOU DIDN'T HAVE TO HEAR HER SCREAM FOR MERCY, YOU DIDN'T HEAR HER BEG, PLEAD, AND GET BURNED ALIVE! Goodbye Lola, I hope you all figure out your war with the gods. I am leaving."

"Leo! YOU CAN'T GO! YOU—"

"I thought you had a boyfriend anyway, so buzz off."

"You're being such a selfish brat! It was Soma! And he died for you. Now you're telling me you won't even try?! I guess everyone was right, Dante must have been crazy; you're a jerk!"

She tried to stop me from leaving, sobbing as she realized I was not willing to risk what was left of my life for their cause.

"LEOOO! PLEASE!! I'M BEGGING YOU! WE NEED YOU! I NEED-"

"BLACKORCHID!"

And with his last words spoken, Leo was gone. He left no indication of what he planned to do, or where he would go. He had abandoned the world that so desperately needed him. Whether it was caused by cowardice or selfishness, he had left them all to fight for themselves. Outnumbered and out muscled they seemed to have had a fictional fragment of a chance left...

CH11: A hopeless world.

Continuing the unholy crusade, kill teams continued to find and imprison all remaining masterminds. Desperately, the masterminds recruited as many new members as possible, even reverting back to the grisly methods that had been used by their predecessors so many years ago. Tens of thousands of innocent people were slaughtered in cold blood to keep the dream of a free world alive. Any angels found responsible for helping Dante's rebellion, as the cause was now referred to, were burned alive and destroyed.

The divine world desperately needed a Savior, they needed Leo, but he had abandoned them. No one had seen or heard from Leo the angel of death in 5 years. Lola had long since become the ring leader in the rebellion. Every day it seemed fewer and fewer were left in Dante's rebellion. Everyone assumed Leo had been killed shortly after walking away from the rebellion; no one had any proof otherwise. They had searched the world over and found no sign of his existence and with the gods ever growing fury unleashed on them; they knew that if something didn't change they would die.

Midtown:

"Look George, I don't care what it takes; I need every mastermind you have in town at the old town theater. We have invested too much in our research there and it's not movable yet.

Word is a kill team will be sent there tomorrow night. We can't lose this. It's our last chance, if they get this it's over."

"I'm sorry Lola; I only have myself and one other guy. Everyone else was caught last week in the midtown raid. They sent 25 kill teams! We didn't stand a chance. I lost so many fine men because of that, they were begging for help that I couldn't give them, it was a slaughter; I barely even made it out!"

"Then it will have to be enough! If this works we might be able to hang on for a little bit longer. Old Town Theater tomorrow at 8am! I have to go see if anyone escaped the Baytown raid."

Baytown:

"Larry? Larry are you there? O god!"

  She screamed in frustration as she walked into the back of the house Larry and 14 other masterminds had been living in. Blood was everywhere and severed fingers and chunks of flesh scattered across the pools of blood.

   "I'm too late...I am so sorry my friends...."

Eastside:

"So why did Lola send me here again buck? Oh right to try and find people who have probably already been caught chopped up and put in a block of concrete? Why don't we just refer to them as killed when that happens?"

"Yeah, I agree.....*aaaaAAAAAAAA*... "

"No! Please, really, I'm just a normal guy, see? HAVE MERCY! Ghlk- ..."

Javax (the rebellion's base of operation):

"Louie get out of there! LOUIE? LOUIE YOU PIECE OF CRAP ANSWER ME... Lola! I think they got Louie...DAMMIT! THEY GOT LOUIE!"

Lola stood there, a tear running down her cheek as she stared at the rebellions motto painted in a huge mural on the wall in front of her.

"When you relish in something that no one else has, you risk being corrupted by it."

At this point corruption was the least of their worries. Sure, they were fighting against corrupt gods, but the main problem they faced now was just staying alive. Her frustration just built more every day. It was far too late to try and make peace with the gods, but something had to change before all that was left of them was a sad story of a crushed rebellion.

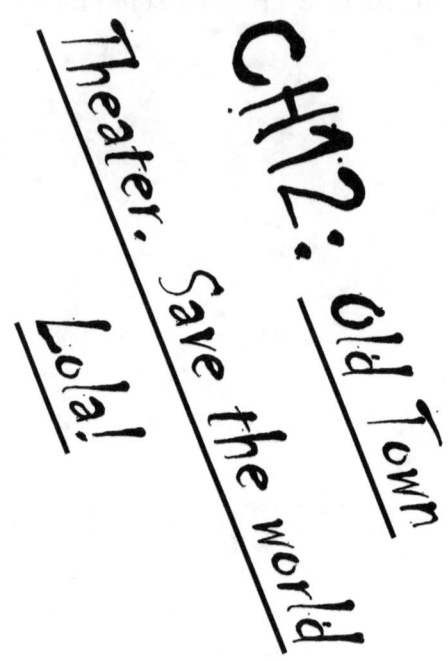

CH12: Old Town

Theater. Save the world

Lola!

The Chronicles of Life and Death.

Old Town Theater: 8am.

"George! Your late, where are you? WHAT!? Dammit George, if they weren't coming before they will be now! Why did you tell him where you were going? I don't know George, you recruited him, maybe you should have known he would turn tail and try to bargain out with the kill team. Don't bother, I am getting out of here before they show up, we will have to start from scratch..."

With a horrific storm of screams outside, Lola quickly realized that no less than 50 kill teams had arrived. Scrambling for what to do next she ran up to the projection room, locking herself in. It would buy her a few minutes at best, but it was better than nothing. She bit her thumb; using the blood she started frantically drawing trigons across the floor. Crash! Out of time! The door came flying in. Dozens of kill team members began pouring in. They were too fast, they pinned her to the wall.

"Lola of the trigon soul, mastermind and recognized leader of Dante's rebellion, for crimes against the gods, including removing death limitations from your own soul, the countless Murder of innocent souls, and plotting against the ring council, you are hereby sentenced to eternal soul prison. Do you have any last words?"

"Yes as a matter of fact! TRAGO MAJESTOS MANISTAS INFINATUM TRIGON!"

All at once the blood she had drawn on the floor began glowing and turned bright red; vaporizing every kill team in the room. But, as she was trying to run out of the room, she was grabbed by the next kill team. Screaming, sobbing, trying to get loose, she realized this might actually be where she died. After all, being dismembered and put into a stone cube for eternity must be death, as she saw it anyway. After 180 years trying to overthrow the gods, had she now lost? Her screaming and sobbing lay unanswered. Her fate seemed all but certain.

"No! Please, you have to understand I am trying to free you all! If I die your hopes of freedom die! Dammit! It can't end here, I CAN'T! NOT LIKE THIS! SOMA!! DANTE!! ANYONE! Help me..." just as it seemed no one would answer something happened, something she didn't expect...the whole building started shaking.

In a thunderous boom, with power she had never heard in any voice, the words echoed clearly through the building.

"AURA DAI MIJA REJUSTAS DELEGRA!!!"

The room was filled with explosions and chaos, someone had just arrived, but she didn't know who. Whoever it was started unleashing a fury of hell upon the kill teams. They scrambled to try and grab him, or physically restrain him otherwise.

Just as fast as her hope had returned, it was leaving her. The kill team finally pinned the mystery man to the floor, piling on to him to stop his rampage. But, her sudden let down was stopped once and for all when she heard him scream out an incant.

"BLACHORCHID!"

Instantly the pile of kill teams that had been on him was gone. He snapped right back into place, but instead of the normal scream from a Wingwave there was a thunderous clap, as if lightning had just struck. It shook the entire building. Lola was speechless. It had to be Leo, but it didn't look, or sound, like him. He was wearing a bright orange cloak that looked like it was made of fire itself. His face was covered with scars, and he had a distant look of sorrow and regret in his now magnificent eyes. There was also a pentagram in each eye. The right eyes pentagram had a brilliant glow, the left eyes was shrouded in a deep shadow.

He stared at her, for no more than a split second, tears falling from his face.

"I'm not too late...Let's go Lola. We have a lot left to do."

CH13: why Leo?! five years of pain, sorrow, and regret.

Snapping into place at Javax, Lola was already sobbing. She started punching and kicking Leo. She was indignant, screaming at him.

"WHY COULDN'T YOU HAVE DONE THIS FIVE YEARS AGO?! YOU ABANDONED US! EVERYONE ELSE IS DEAD NOW!! HOW COULD YOU HAVE JUST LEFT US?! HOW COULD YOU HAVE JUST LEFT ME?!"

Despite all of this, he maintained an eerie calmness in his presence. Listening to every name she called him and taking every punch and kick she threw. Only after she had finally wound down did he say anything.

"Not everyone Lola, I don't have time to explain everything that happened, but we have help now. Saris can you hear me? Yes this is Leo. Expect our arrival; remove the Wingwave seal so we can snap in. Lola, forgive my rush, but grab what you need, I will show you what will soon be our salvation."

Once again taking her hand, hey shout the pass phrase in his booming voice. In an instant the world around them began to look as if it was on fire. This was not Wingwave, at least not that of an angel.

"Forgive me Lola; this may get a little hot"

As he said that, it seemed an infernal blaze was lit around them. The vortex of fire spun faster and faster, until, they snapped into a giant pentagram drawn on a cave floor. This was no cave however; this was a cathedral, a palace. The walls were constructed from a dark crystal. Ornate symbols decorated the ceiling. A giant candle chandelier was hanging high above them with the flames burning black.

"Leo what on earth is this place? Where have you brought me?!

"Welcome to hell Lola. This is Hades."

She instantly flipped from calm to an extreme panic; trying to get away from him.

"You're in cahoots with the god of death?! Why Leo?! What happened to-?"

He put a finger to her lips, and a hand on her shoulder.

"I am the god of death now Lola, I killed the last one. Hell is now my domain. And the residents of hell, banished forever from heaven, are more than happy to help us with our cause. Dante's rebellion not only lives on, now it has a chance! I am sorry it took so long Lola, but I did come back for you!"

"5 years too late! You jerk! I watched everyone around me die. Do you know how many people died because of you? I lost everything... "

"Not everything Lola."

She froze, as she realized who had just spoken. She turned slowly to see Dante leaning against a wall.

Just as she was finally about to say something, they were interrupted.

"Sir we have a situation, the XO team you sent to retrieve the artifact from Leis Temple has been tracked by a kill team, they need help sir!"

"Forgive me Lola; we will have to talk later. Scramble my personal team; we are going to save them! Dante please show her around and answer what you can for her."

A team of 10 men ran up, stopped, saluted, and spoke in unison.

"Sir!"

Leo grabbed a scroll of paper and stuffed it into his cloak. Asking if they were ready, he checked that everyone was there. They then headed back toward the giant pentagram on the floor he had arrived on, and in an instant they were gone.

Dante pushed off the wall and started walking, signaling for Lola to follow him. He walked her through the entire base. They had everything, a giant dining hall, a room as big as a football field with what appeared to be maps of the mortal plain, and among other things, a huge store of divine weapons.

Dante explained to her that they had figured out how to use the sonic frequency generated from a weapon firing to make a sort of pseudo incantation. They adjusted the riffling of the barrel and engraved certain patterns on the outside of the bullet, causing the air spinning around it to focus the energy for the incant. Now even the average citizen of hell who wasn't able to verbally cast an incantation could fight back against the Ring gods.

"Dante, that's great, it really is, but how? How are you even here right now? What happened?! What happened to Leo?"

"The book Lola; not the chronicles, there is another book. It is called The Immortal Soul. Leo used it to bring me back. In this book the soul of everyone ever turned into an angel is sealed. He unsealed my soul and used an incredibly powerful incantation. He was able to bring me back from the shadows."

"But what happened to him Dante? How did he get all this power? Why now?"

"I don't even know what happened to him Lola, but the Leo we have now has already killed one god, and is on track to kill all the ring gods. He is collecting ancient artifacts that will enable us to destroy the rest of them! He is my dream envisioned..."

"Dante, I was left alone for 5 years watching everything fall apart. Everyone we had rounded up is dead. Forgive my doubtfulness here, but what's going to protect us when the ring council figures out his plan? I refuse to watch everyone die again."

"Lola, this time we will win! They haven't even figured out we are doing anything. And when they do, we will crush them! I will have my revenge and after hundreds of years we will finally be free!"

She smiled, but inside she was crying, she didn't want to lose anyone else. She worried that Dante was now obsessed with revenge, not liberation. Why had they left everyone in the old rebellion behind? Why didn't he seem to care that she had nearly died? Was his hatred so great that it had replaced his compassion?

CH14: The great war begins.

"Half of you take the east half of the temple, the rest of you with me. We need to find that XO team time now. Move out!"

Armed with the new weapons they looked like, no, they were Dante's army. They moved with speed, precision, and purpose conducting a grid sweep of the entire area leaving no stone un-turned.

"Sir, there is nobody here, sir."

Despite their effort they had found no trace of the XO team or the artifact. Leo was starting to question if it was ever there in the first place, or if it had been an elaborate trap all along. In a furious storm of screams he got his answer.

No less than 100 kill teams appeared, surrounding them. A brutal fight erupted, but the sheer number of kill teams was quickly overwhelming them. Even Leo had seemed to reach his limit. To make matters worse the kill teams had started using Leo's old tactics, grabbing someone and flying out with wing wave. After a massive struggle, only Leo was left, fighting them.

"Dante can you hear me? No matter what happens don't send anyone! It won't make a difference...I will destroy them all on my own."

"GRAN MAJOS, RAIN OF DESTRUCTIOP!"

In a huge squeal, and thunderous boom, everything in a two square mile radius was gone. The explosion left only a crater. Standing in the middle of this hellish landscape, Leo held his arms skyward and screamed in a thunderous rage.

"You can send all you want, I will destroy them! As soon as I finish finding what I need, your lot is next! I will destroy you for what you have taken from me!!"

"Saris, I am returning, remove the seals. Saris are you there? SARIS?!"

"Leo, you've really done it now haven't you?"

Her sweet voice instantly paralyzed him; he turned to see RUNA standing before him.

"Why did you leave me to die Leo? Did I mean so little to you?"

But he knew the answer; he felt so much guilt over leaving her it had drove him to make a deal with the Devil himself. In exchange for 5 years of loyal service to hell, he was taught to incant and given "The Immortal Soul". He turned his back on those who needed him because he was unwilling to give her up. He loved her and He had done everything to bring her back, until to his horror he had found out she never was an angel. Her soul was not contained in the book.

At the end of the book was signed: "—Runa6. God of life, creator of angels, commander of kill corps." She had been the one who had turned Dante into an angel, as a result stealing Leo's life as well. He learned she alone was also in charge of the kill teams. She had faked her own death, knowing he would be driven to try and save her. She knew he had grown fond of her in the short time they had known each other.

His hatred of her had only grown when he found out, at the end of his 5 years serving the king of hell, that all of this had been done to keep the Savior of Dante's rebellion out of the way. He had become so enraged, that with a single word the power of his soul had directed enough energy to destroy the god of death, at the cost of greatly weakening of his power. After that he brought back Dante using the immortal soul, rallied the denizens of hell for their cause, promised Dante his revenge, and sought out Lola, who he had abandoned. He had only just been able to save her, but he wanted to make things right. It was he, who had abandoned them all.

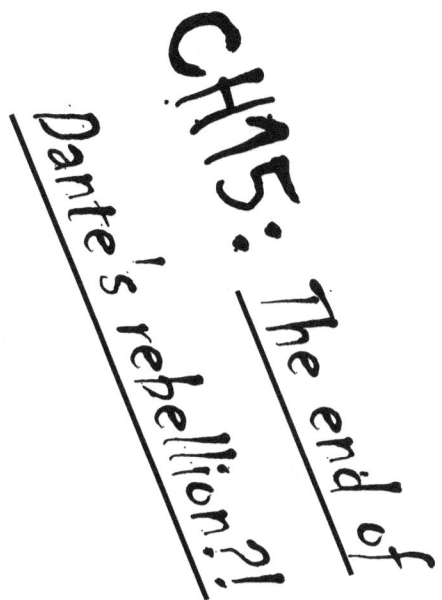

CH15: The end of Dante's rebellion?!

"Leo, why won't you answer me? We did you leave me to die?"

Her smile and laugh now seemed more twisted than sweet.

"Oh calm down Leo, I am not here to kill you, not yet. I just thought I should tell you that we have killed everyone in hell. You walked right into our trap, and because of you, everyone's dead. You look angry I think we will have to talk more after you have had a chance to cool off."

He was in fact outraged, he had fallen for her trick again, but he couldn't muster the nerve to kill her. His heart still reminded him of his love for her. His brain told him it was pointless, just kill her. But he couldn't do it. As he stood there, trying to overcome his inability to strike her, she leaned in, gave him one passionate kiss and disappeared.

He made his way back to hell by Wingwave. The seals had been burned; the residents of hell had been massacred just as she said. He had let down everyone who had looked to him for leadership. Because of him, they had died. Lola and Dante, who he was trying to make up for abandoning, had paid the price. His new kingdom was now filled only with the charred remains of those he alone was supposed to save.

On his knees, he stared at the floor, crying. He had nothing left to fight for. He was questioning what he should do... Should he just give up to Runa, try to beg for her mercy? As horrible as that sounded to him, she was all he had left...

"You know it's not very becoming for the god of death to be seen crying, it makes you seem pretty weak. Keep your chin up Mr. Leon, the plain of the mortals still needs you."

Wait, he recognized that voice, that sly hint of a smile emanating in the tone. Quickly standing up, none other than John Divine was there in front of him. Same old sly smile plastered across his face, and pleasant demeanor to boot. But how was he there? Leo was at a loss as to what was going on.

"Mr. Leon I still don't have time to fully explain, but if it will put your mind at ease, imagine if you will the space between the mortal plain, and the higher plane. I sealed my soul in that limbo of non-existence. There are only certain times I can correctly concentrate the energy from there to project myself to other plains since Dante destroyed my body.

Dante and Lola are not dead. Lola helped him become a mastermind since he had a soul now; unfortunately they had to use some of the citizens of hell to be able to quickly achieve this feat. They were both taken to soul prison. If you wish to save them you will have to give up all of the power you have gained in order to free them.

You will need to go to the higher plain, the realm of the divine ring. The only way to get there at the moment will open at noon tomorrow, and closes at midnight. The entrance I am working on is located in the Sauldaday crypt.

If and when you are able to get to the stone cubes imprisoning Dante and Lola, use this incant: "Cruxa soul demanos, sacris de vigor!" Only use that twice Leo. It will use the energy of your soul to break the incantation binding the essence of their soul into the stone. If you use it any more than twice it will destroy your soul. Time's up, good luck Leo, I have faith in you to do the right thing!"

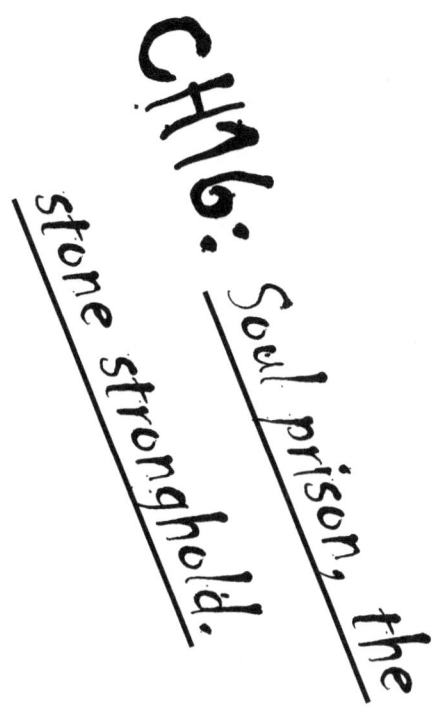

CH16: Soul prison, the stone stronghold.

Leo left behind everything he had worked for, returning to where he had walked away, to Javax. This time he was determined to make things right. He wouldn't fall for another trick. This would end one way or the other. At least if he failed, he hadn't walked away this time. He was ready to do whatever it took to be the Savior everyone had expected him to be from the start, no matter what the cost.

Surveying the scene, it was just as they had left it when he brought Lola to hades. Had he left her here she would have been fine...his power had blinded him to his weakness. This was his entire fault. Crying, he looked up to see the mural: "When you relish in something no one else has, you risk being corrupted by it." How true it seemed to him. Had he stayed in hades, he might have been able to help them. His overconfidence had led him right into a trap.

He stayed the night at Javax, finally falling asleep. He had nightmares of the thing the death god had made him do. Nightmares of the things he had seen. But most of all, he had nightmares of when he walked away from Lola for his own selfish desires, leaving her to watch a failing rebellion and the death of those around her. He saw her crying, screaming, and begging him to stay, over and over.

Awaking the next morning he felt the strain of his restless sleep. Today was the day he would make everything right. He began writing up scrolls of various auto incantations, as he had learned to do in his time away. Hopefully these would help him get past the security they would most likely have. He left only a sealed note on Lola's desk.

He then grabbed his cloak, and set off for the
Sauldaday Crypt. No use lingering around Javax any
longer. Upon his arrival it seemed as though nothing
had changed in the last five years, except for an extra
layer of dust. He stood where he had as Runa had been
instructing him, before he had learned of her twisted
plans. Trying to block the thoughts from his head, he
was starting to worry. The kiss only proved it; he was,
at some point, going to have an issue killing her. His
infatuation with her had already stopped him once, and
the kiss only made things worse. As sinister and
manipulative as she had turned out to be, he still
wanted to be with her, he still loved her.

Finally the time was at hand, a loud rip as time and
space separated before him. He saw a shining city.
Unmistakably, in the middle was a stone tower of
monstrous proportions. This upper plain, the divine
world, was absolutely huge. It was easily a thousand

times the size of hades, and he had not yet even left the main courtyard of the stronghold. Hades was rumored to be 15 million square miles. He could only imagine how big, in total, this plain of existence was.

He stepped through this rift into the upper plain. The light seemed to burn at his skin. Spending so much time in hell was probably causing his adverse reaction. No time to worry about that, he set out toward the stone stronghold. Passing thru the divine city, he was met with fear. People ran into their houses, presumably never seeing such a person walking through the streets of heaven; his bright orange cloak blazing against the normal backdrop of their world. And they were right to fear him, he was on a mission. If someone got in his way now he would destroy them.

Something wasn't right; surely they had noticed a rift into their plain. Why had the ring council, or Runa, not sent anyone to respond? Was this a trap as well? No time to think about it, this was his only chance to save Lola. It took the better part of 3 hours walking to reach the stone tower. Upon reaching it he was shocked to find, yet again, and alarming lack of security. No door and no guards. This reeked of a trap, was john divine in on it? Or was something else entirely going on?

CH17: Stonewalled.

Right as he was about to walk into the building, he heard the voice of a small boy.

"I wouldn't do that mister. Anyone doing that wouldn't survive. See that symbol above the door?"

He threw a rock through the doorway, as it cleared the threshold; it began to disintegrate into dust.

"See! I told ya. If you wanna go play on the rocks I can show you the other way in."

He began running around the tower. Leo quickly took off behind him, trying to keep pace with the energetic young boy. Finally, the boy stopped, pushed on a seemingly solid part of the wall, and pointed inside.

"This is the door they use when they bring those big rocks in mister."

Leo thanked the boy and sent him on his way. He then entered through the passage, as soon as he entered the door slammed shut, once again leaving what seemed to be a solid wall. Hopefully he would be able to find it again when it was time to leave.

Surveying the area he was almost disappointed in its sheer simplicity. There were thick stone walls and floors illuminated by floating candles, a staircase leading up to the next level, and stone cubes scattered across the outer perimeter. On each cube there was a name engraved, below the name was a list of crimes. This was beginning to look like it would take quite a while. Maybe not, logically speaking, perhaps since this room appeared to be completely filled with stone cubes, Maybe they filled from the bottom floor to the top floor? It was worth a shot.

He began going up, floor by floor. Every room looked almost identical and he still wasn't sure if the lack of security was a blessing, or something more malevolent.

He began to lose count of the cubes. Thousands of masterminds lay entrapped before him in stone cubes. He wished he could save them all, but he knew he could only use this incantation to break the cube twice; once for Lola, and once for Dante.

Reaching the top floor he ran into a new problem, above the doorway leading in was the same symbol from the entrance. He could clearly see three stone cubes sitting on the far wall; it must have been Lola, Dante, and someone else. But how could he get through the doorway?

He pulled out one of the scrolls of paper he had with him and held it to the wall next to the door. It had a circular pattern of writing on it. He taped it and spoke an incantation.

"Reshavos de amuzo!"

The symbols on the paper began spinning, the circle becoming a blur, spinning until the wall itself started to disappear behind it leaving a hole in the wall. Now he had a way in.

CH18: Leonardo's decision.

He cautiously entered the room and was disappointed once again at the lack of any real security.

"I thought this was a prison!"

He mused to himself. Secretly glad at the ease he had getting here. He read the names off the cubes, Dante, Lola, and SOMA!? This was an unforeseen turn of events, but he could only use the incant twice.

He quickly set to work, going first to Dante's stone cube. Preparing himself for the worst he held his hands over the cube, clearing his mind he spoke the words required of him.

"Cruxa soul demanos, sacris de vigor!"

He instantaneously felt crippling pain run throughout his body. Fighting it, he began to realize what was happening. This wasn't just removing the stone; it was using his divine energy to mend them back together.

Unfortunately, the divine energy was fused with his soul and his natural energy; it being ripped out was the worse pain he had ever felt.

After what seemed like an eternity to Leo, around 5 minutes in reality, Dante was standing in front of him, completely restored to his pre Stone Age persona.

"How is this possible? Was I not encased by the ring gods? How am I here right now Leo, what have you done? "

"Don't ask Dante. Right now all I am worried about is getting Lola free and you both out of here in one piece."

He moved to her cube, once again saying the words required to initiate the incantation.

"Cruxa soul demanos, sacris de vigor!!"

The pain was tenfold this time, it was far greater than he had expected and he was left on the ground writhing. Dante grabbed his arm and pulled him up; to his relief Lola was now standing in front of them. Overwhelmed Leo burst into tears, he apologized for leaving them, before collapsing again.

Lola caught him, exclaiming how stupid he was for saving her, but thanked him none the less.

"Leo! What price have you paid to free us?!"

Looking over him he had changed. His eyes had returned to their normal shade, the pentagrams had faded away. His voice had become softer, weaker; He was a mortal once more.

"What have you done now Leo...?"

She asked as she held him, the concern evident in her eyes.

"I am the hope Lola, so I did something hopeful."

He said with a sheepish smile. Soon he was standing back up, a little worse for wear and mortal, but he was back up on his own two feet.

He told them to go on ahead of him; there was no security in here aside from the two trap doorways. He also told them about the secret passage to leave the tower and about the rift to return to the mortal plain. He had one more thing he needed to check before he could leave.

After making sure they had left, he walked over to Soma's cube.

"Lola needs you now friend. I have outlived my usefulness, and quite honestly I think I just made it worse for everyone."

"CRUXA SOUL DEMANOS, SACRIS DE VIGOR!"

The pain this time was even worse than the last two times, it felt as though his soul itself was being ripped out, and maybe it was. This time it must be using the last reserves of his soul's energy. Just as soma was getting up, Dante ran back into the room. He caught Leo as he collapsed.

"Why Leo? Why did you do this?! Do you realize you just used your own soul to free him?!"

"Dante, after you brought me into all of this I resented it all, I hated what you had done to me, but I never hated you. You are the one who wanted revenge, so you will have to get it yourself. You and Lola both loved Soma, your brother, and her love. He will be more help than I could be...Dante I couldn't kill Runa, the god responsible for all of this. Yes it was her! I had the chance, but I couldn't lift a finger against her. I think I loved her Dante...I know it's silly, but I just couldn't do it."

The look on Dante's face betrayed his emotions, a look of great sorrow as the tears fell from his face.

"But you were the hope of everyone Leo; I can't do this without you. I didn't save you as a child, watch you grow up, to watch you kill yourself. Dammit Leo! You have to live! Lola loved you; Soma was never more than a friend to her. SHE *LOVED YOU!*"

"I am sorry Dante, I loved Runa. She was the enemy, and I would only stop your dream. Take your brother and Lola and get your revenge with your own hands. And thank you, despite everything, if it hadn't been for you I would've never been on this splendid adventure. It was really..."

"He's dead Dante. I am sorry brother; I know how much faith you had in him and how you treated him as your own. Let's go brother."

Soma's words were both sobering and devastating. Dante had indeed placed all of his faith in Leo. Without Leo he wasn't sure what to do. He had no backup plan.

CH18.5: Tears from heaven.

Soma and Dante walked out of the stone tower, carrying Leo's corpse. Tears still streaming down Dante's face, as if the son he never got to have died. Lola had a mixed reaction as they walked out. Soma, her old friend, was free. But Leo, the hope of everyone, the person she had secretly loved had sacrificed everything to do that. The happiness was quickly replaced by tears as she saw Leo's lifeless corpse.

"What have you done now Leo? This was just stupid, not hopeful. I loved you. Soma was a dear friend, but I lied to you because I was afraid after everything you'd been through you wouldn't love me. I watched you every day when you came to buy coffee. I only lived above the shop, but they let me make coffee for you every day because they knew I had a crush on you. Every time you would almost ask me out I had wished you did. The one time you did, when I shot you down, I was joking. I loved you Leo. DAMMIT LEO!

Why did you have to break my heart twice..." She spoke, wishing he could hear her, the sorrow of her voice portraying her ruptured heart.

A sudden storm of screams, it was the kill teams! The luxury of time was no longer there. They left Leo's body, and ran through town, toward the rift.

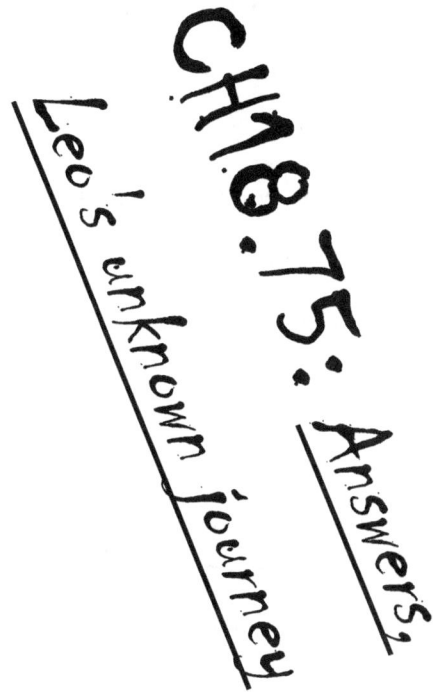

CH18.75: Answers,

Leo's unknown journey

Dante, Lola, and Soma returned to Javax. They were all at a loss as to what would happen next. They were free to start plotting there next move, but it just seemed too soon. Leo's death was weighing on both Dante and Lola. And still the corrupted gods of the world remained, untouched. Dante never told Lola that Leo had fallen over there enemy, Runa, she had suffered enough for now.

Going through her desk trying to find anything useful for what to do next, she saw the note Leo had left her.

"You'll find the Chronicles of hell in the plain of hades, the royal throne room. Forgive me for what I am about to do Lola. I will miss you."

Crying again she rushed to show the note to Dante and Soma. They all agreed that they would go to hell to

get this book. Whatever it was, Leo clearly wanted
them to have it.

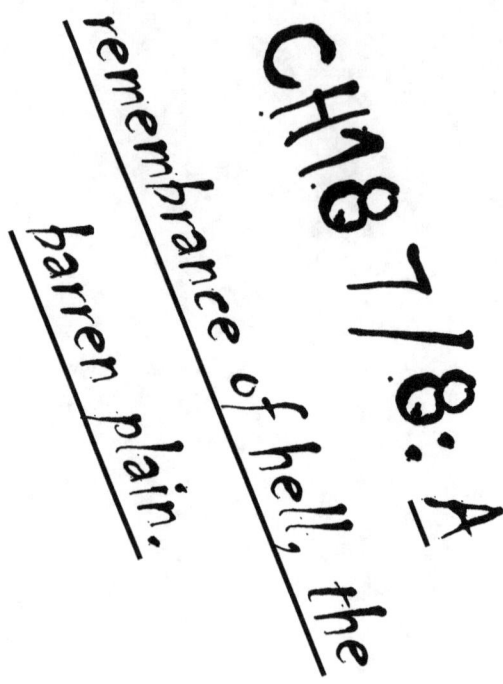

CH18 7/8: A remembrance of hell, the barren plain.

Upon arriving in hell, the events that had transpired here was still fresh in their memories.

They had been talking, awaiting Leo's return, when a giant crash and torrent of screams shattered the peace. Hundreds of kill teams began snapping into place. Everyone scrambled for weapons, trying to hold off the army that had begun attacking them. Lola and Dante were the last to fall. They fought off the onslaught as long as they could, but the residents of hell were no match for the sheer number of kill teams.

Upon finally being restrained, they were read their crimes. Lola had to watch as Dante, who had become a mastermind after being brought back with his soul, was first. She heard him try to muffle his own screams as they brutally chopped his tongue, arms, and legs off. Then, holding up a finger and lighting him on fire with the divine flame, Dante saw one last glimpse of life before the flames solidified into a stone cube.

She tried to brace herself for it, but the pain was too intense. She began screaming as they dismembered her. The fire burning her flesh as it engulfed her made her wish she had been mortal so she could just die; surely a shot to the head was better than this. And then the horrific feeling, as the flames wrapped around her, turning to stone. She couldn't see, hear, smell, or speak. She was just there. She would spend an eternity of existing without purpose.

Un-aware of how much time was passing, she had felt as if an eternity had passed before Leo had freed her. The whole time he was the only thing she was thinking about. She wondered if he would even remember her, or

L&D The Chronicles of Life and Death.

if he had become so powerful that an insignificant girl like her would even matter to him.

She snapped out of her reminiscing as Dante grabbed her shoulder, asking her if she would like to help look for the book.

They soon found the chronicles of hell and also made sure to grab the immortal soul before returning to Javax. They didn't want to stay in hell any longer than necessary.

CH19: Hell, in a hand basket.

After returning from hell they began reading the chronicles of hell. It was a compendium of events from the last five years that Leo had written, his journal. In it were un-evenly spaced entries of the major events of the five years prior. Sometimes there were entries every day, other times maybe one or two a month. However it brought light to his obsession with getting back Runa. The god of death had promised him a book that could bring back any angel that had been destroyed. Using their soul and an incantation they would be reborn as a mortal, "The Immortal Soul".

In his entries he also recorded the deep regret he had for leaving everyone behind, and on many days he wished he could have broken his agreement and gone to help them. It also had many hand written notes into the various incants and other magical things he had learned. How to seal an incant into a scroll for later use, Summoning things from another plain of existence using pentagramax, and the secrets he was learning about non-verbal incantation. Dante was making notes of all the various incants and tricks and soma was putting together a timeline of events, but Lola had stopped listening. She had loved him, but it appeared that he had never returned the affection. Instead he just had regrets of leaving her, presumably to die.

The last pages he had written were of his rage. After serving for five years, the god of death had made good on his word, giving Leo the book. Leo however, felt he had been tricked. No matter how many times he looked at it, Runa's soul was not in the book. It wasn't that there were pages missing, it just wasn't there.

He had marched to the god of death and demanded the real book. That Runa's soul was not present. The god of death merely brushed him off.

"If her soul is not in the book, she either wasn't dead, or was never an angel."

Leo had been so enraged by this that he had manifested a huge amount of power and, in his anger, killed the god of death. But after reading these notes, his journal, they couldn't help but feel perhaps the god of death had not been so bad after all. Sure some of the things he had Leo do were not favorably, or inherently good, but they were far from evil. He had been a just ruler of hades and had kept peace there. He had never done anything to the mortal realm except offer a safe haven to those the heavens would not take. He gave them a home, and genuinely seemed to care, despite the iron fist image he portrayed to them.

While they had trusted Leo's judgment on everything else, they began to see a darker side of him. It was ruled by his anger and obsession with Runa. They had a new understanding of why he had sacrificed himself. He was so obsessed with her; he may very well have turned on them to save her, the corrupted god of the world. He had written so many times: "Never again will I abandon my friends." And he knew that he could not trust himself around her, even after finding out she was evil. So he made sure, for his friends sake that it could never happen. He had given up his life in order that they may have a shot to stop her. It was a long shot, but it was better than nothing.

CH20: Dante's dream.

That night, as Dante dreamed, he had nightmares of his past. Taken from heaven by a team of men in bright white cloaks, he had begged and pleaded to stay. He just wanted to see his brother when he died and came to heaven.

But they wouldn't even listen, dragging him to a stone room where a tall being, divine in nature, was slumped over on the ground. He presumed this man was dying but had no idea why he had been brought there. They put a stone cross around his neck, tied his hands behind his back, and locked him in the room. After the other man had passed on, slowly disappearing into the shadows, Dante began feeling a horrific tearing sensation all across his body. Wrenching on the floor it lasted for hours until they finally opened the door as it was subsiding.

"Angelic conversion was successful; his soul has been sealed away."

He heard them say while opening the door. They grabbed him and took him to another room, locking him up again and they just left him there.

As he laid on the floor crying, he wondered why this was happening to him, he had done nothing wrong. He just wanted to see his brother again, to tell him he forgave him for everything that had happened.

His dream suddenly shifted back to the days when he was alive. He had been very close to his brother, having lost their parents at a young age; they only had each other to rely on. They were fiercely competitive, but no matter who ended up winning, at the end of the day, they were always brothers first. Growing up with no parents, they mostly had to steal, it was better than starving. They worked for food and shelter whenever they could, but work was scarce for street kids.

No matter what happened, they never blamed each other. They promised no matter what, if anything happened they would always be there to save one another. Their bond alone you could have written a book over, until the one day the brothers became obsessed with a girl. They began to drift apart, the unbreakable bond they had shared dissolving into the shadows of jealousy.

The girls name was Lola. They had both met her in the market, both instantly being taken aback by her. She had been a beauty in every respect, and a thief as well. She also grew up as a vagabond with no parents. She was smart and strong, easily able to keep up with the hijinks the brothers pulled every day. All three of them spent most of the free time they had together, even as they competed for her affection. They both knew a girl like her was one of a kind, they also realized that one of them would end up alone not matter what happened.

Fighting over her, the girl they had both dreamed about for so long. Their bond diminished, the brothers kept drifting further apart, until one day, while stealing food in the market the angry stall owner had managed to catch Dante.

"Soma, brother! Help me!"

He begged as soma ran away, looking back only once, not knowing the full situation he had left his brother in. This vigilante merchant was so tired of kids stealing from him that he decided to use Dante as an example. He killed Dante, leaving his body in the middle of the market. Under the law of the land anyone caught stealing was subject to whatever punishment those he stole from saw fit to bestow.

The next day Soma and Lola had gone back to the city, and found the message left for them. Soma's heart sank deep as he realized what had happened, he had left his brother to die. Lola had scolded him the night before, asking how he could have left his brother there. She asking what happened to them, they used to be so close.

"It was you Lola, we both loved you! Can't you see?!"

But she couldn't understand, because while she may have been their friend, she had never cared for them in the same manner. All of the fighting had been for nothing. The magnitude of this had left a lasting scar on Soma. He left town, not seen for years, blaming himself for his brother's death. He refused to move on. He had slowly descended into a state of insanity. Living in a cave with nobody else around for miles, he began losing touch with reality. He began having delusions, his brother's image haunting his mind.

All the while, in heaven where he was able to look down and watch his brother, Dante instead blamed himself. Had he not been so obsessed with Lola, he wouldn't have driven his brother to insanity. He longed for nothing more than to tell his brother he that it wasn't his fault, to live his life instead of wasting away.

But the days drew on and he had become further depressed as his brother became less in touch with reality. Sometimes reaching out, crying and screaming to go back and change what had happened. He was forever stuck reliving that day and no amount of screaming at him would change that, but he had long since past the point of reason. Dante continued to watch his brother, until the day he was taken from heaven.

He found out he had been turned into the next angel of death, that they had sealed away his soul. That he would never see his brother again, in the mortal plain or the divine plain. Anger filled his being; he swore revenge on the gods that had done this to him. He would bide his time until he could destroy them! He would make them pay for what they had done to him.

Years after his death, and after acquiring experience collecting the souls of mortals, he came upon a group of men, brilliant men. They agreed that it probably was there time to go, but asked him if maybe they could stay just a little longer. They explained they were close to finishing a book that could remove death limitations from the soul. If he let them finnish the book, they would give it to him to use as he wished. Seeing the opportunity to one day be able to see his brother again he agreed. He told them an incant to use against him so that the gods wouldn't know of his treachery. They sealed the deal in a blood oath, and used the incantation on Dante. All he could hope was that his brother could hold some sliver of sanity until he got the book to him.

Sure enough, as soon as they completed it, they gave it to him. Only one was present and accepting his end, helped to cast the second incant, allowing him to kill them, once more. The others however he hadn't heard from for a couple of weeks, presumably trying not to honor the agreement.

The ring council, outrage that anyone had tricked death, made him focus solely on tracking down these immortal beings, unaware of the book, or Dante being fully responsible for this. He agreed for now, biding his time, still hoping his brother would hang on long enough to be saved.

Five more years had passed, until finally he had a chance to find his brother, sent to collect the soul of a nearby villager. He walked into the cave his brother had called home. Crying as he saw his brother, lying on the floor, curled into a ball. He called out to Soma, but he was so far gone that he didn't even seem to hear.

"Soma, it's your brother! Do you remember me?"

I CAN'T SAVE YOU BROTHER, I FAILED YOU, LEAVE ME ALONE, JUST LEAVE ME ALONE!!!

Soma screamed back at him, rocking back and forth, crying. He must have thought it was just another voice tormenting his poor soul. It broke Dante's heart to see all the pain he had caused his brother. He grabbed Soma's shoulder, speaking softer, in a tone full of his own remorse.

"Brother, forgive me. Forgive me for leaving you for all these years, please brother come back to me...I never blamed you brother! It was MY fault. Not yours! But I need you to come back to me"

Soma raised his head, the tears streaming down his face. "Brother!" He jumped up and hugged Dante as hard as he could. "I'm so sorry brother, so sorry..." sobbing as he spoke.

Soma, my time here is short, I brought you this book. I know that the methods are unthinkable, but I need you brother. I need you to live! If it takes 500 years I will find a way to be there for you again. Soma took the book, flipping thru the pages, he didn't notice Dante leave.

Soma spent the Next 500 years killing. The first life he took brought him great sorrow, he couldn't believe what he had just done, but he had to keep moving forward. He soon became immortal, and he was determined to make sure he saw his brother again. He became numb to the fact of that he was ending so many innocent lives. He would one day see his brother again. But his cold hearted killing didn't go unnoticed. His cold hearted acts earned him a nickname... Mr. Mittens: Lest anyone touch someone so cold without a pair of mittens.

500 years later, unknown to John Divine, Dante had no intention of killing Soma, Mr. Mittens. He had been lying to the ring council for the past few hundred years claiming to have been just now learning information about this book. They charged Dante with finding, and imprisoning him. He was able to convince the ring council to spare soma this fate, in exchange for his power being sealed, and him handing over the book. Soma delightfully accepted. He had lied to Leo when he said the wounds were from Mr. Mittens. He had really self-inflicted the wounds, so that Leo, the hope of the world, could become angelic. To pass on his powers, he had to die.

CH21: Delusions of grandeur.

Dante was abruptly woken up by Lola; something was wrong with Soma. She had woken him up in a craze, talking about some little man who had shown up and told him to go to a mountain before it was too late. He had told her to see for herself, he was in the next room. However, when she checked no one was there. He swore up and down that he wasn't crazy and started frantically searching for the man he had seen; but he was nowhere to be found.

Dante wasn't sure what was going on, but of all times why now? Couldn't he have held on to his sanity for just a little longer? The ring gods would be bearing down on them at any moment, and they had no trump card, Leo was dead and they weren't sure what to do now. Why had he suddenly just snapped out of his mind?

The whole world seemed to be falling apart around them, but he was at least determined to keep the three of them together for as long as possible and to do that they had to find Soma.

"Come on Lola, we better go find him before the Ring Gods do, I don't want to lose my brother again!"

They searched for him the entire night, never finding a single trace as to where he had gone. With no clue what exactly had happened to him, or where he may have gone, the situation was just getting worse. The tension between Dante and Lola was growing by the hour. She kept telling him that Soma knew what he was doing; he would be fine. But Dante could tell something else was going on, Soma never lost his mind; he was too smart for that. Dante had to make sure he was ok.

So they followed the only lead they had at the time; go to a mountain.

Unfortunately there were numerous mountains around them; they didn't have the luxury of being able to go search them all. Furthermore, for all they knew, the ring council had already got to him. They searched as many as they could, but after hours upon hours of nothing they reluctantly returned to Javax, being careful to make sure no one followed them. The way things had been going they could have searched for weeks and found nothing.

Lola spent most of the night trying to cheer up Dante; his mood had been horrible since Soma disappeared. She could tell that's all he was thinking about and nothing she said seemed to be able to change that. His dark mood seemed to be contagious, plunging her into darker thoughts. She began to wonder what happened to someone when there soul was destroyed. As far as they knew, there were only three plains of existence. There was the mortal realm, hades, and the divine plain.

But, she wondered, what happened to the destroyed souls? Were they really gone forever? Would she truly never see Leo again? She was almost back to the point of tears, but attempted to hold it together for Dante's sake.

Dante meanwhile had been pondering what could've caused Soma to go crazy. Why had he left without saying anything to him? Where did his brother go? Most importantly, he was trying to figure out the next move. As far as he could tell there was now only the two of them, against the entire Ring army. The needed something, some kind of advantage to stand any shadow of a chance. The two of them against an army, no matter how he looked at it, it wasn't looking good.

Lola had gone to the kitchen, to make more tea, when she suddenly burst back into the room. She began telling Dante that soma really hadn't been crazy! A strange little man had just appeared out of nowhere, told her not to worry about soma, and said to go to the Sauldaday crypt tomorrow. He had said his name was John Divine. Dante thought she had lost her mind too, but checked anyway.

Once again no one else had been in the kitchen. Besides John Divine couldn't be here, Dante had killed Him with his own hands. He began to wonder what exactly she had put in her tea, or if this was some sort of a trick from the ring gods. Something really wasn't right here, but he couldn't figure out what it was. He felt like all the pieces to the puzzle where there, they just weren't fitting together.

He told her to calm down, but she was adamant; there would be something that could help them at the crypt tomorrow. She couldn't explain it without sounding crazy, but She was going whether he went with her or not. He didn't have much of a choice, trap or not, he couldn't leave her on her own if something happened. He didn't like it, but he agreed to go with her. Even if it was a trap, it was better than doing nothing...

CH22: The Nexus plain.

In total darkness, a young man woke up completely dazed. Unsure of what was happening, he questioned aloud to himself, as if to expect some sort of answer.

"Where am I? What is this place?"

The more important question child is who are you said a soft voice in the darkness. And what are you, Said another voice in a deeper tone. Even more important yet, why are you, asked a third voice in a more serious tone. Then, they spoke in unison, addressing the entire matter at hand.

"You must answer these questions before we can answer your questions young one."

"But I don't remember who, what, or why I am. I don't remember anything, nothing at all."

He was becoming frustrated; no matter how much he tried he couldn't remember anything.

That just won't do, said one voice. Not at all, said another. The third voice then said: perhaps he isn't the one; perhaps we have made a mistake. The other two quickly bellowed back in unison, we three do not make mistakes!! Well then we must help him to remember his purpose, am I correct, Asked the third voice. Yes! Very much so, agreed the other two. They decided they would help him to remember who, what, and why he was. For only after he was whole once more, could they unleash him on that accursed Runa! Her treachery was unforgivable; she would pay the highest cost.

"Excuse me, if I could possibly interrupt your conversation for a moment, mysterious voices, is there anything any of you three can recommend to help me remember? What can I do? I really don't like being so confused about anything; about everything..."

Yes! Very much so! Absolutely! The three voices said in there now familiar order.

"You must go through the light, to the mountain, and only if you can reach the peak, you will remember. We will await your return here. But, beware for the risk is great. Though the reward is greater, if you let your guard down for but a moment, the mountain will completely destroy you! GO NOW, if you dare..."

As they commanded him to leave, a bright light appeared on the horizon. The young man ran toward it, quickly crossing into what seemed like a lush forest directly after he entered the light. Had it been like this the entire time? No, it couldn't have been.

Directly in from of him was a giant mountain. At the base was a red gate with words engraved on the top. It read: "O ye lost soul, before you is certain doom. Turn back or risk being lost forever."

"Charming."

He mused to himself, attempting to remain undaunted. He walked through the gate, following what seemed to be the trail to the top, unsure if this would really help or if he would end up lost forever. He at least had to try, otherwise what was the point? In his current state he couldn't remember anything. At least this way he had some sort of chance to remember something.

After a few hours he soon realized this mountain seemed to have a will of its own; unlike any mountain he had ever stepped foot on before. It wanted to destroy him; he could feel its malevolent will.

Segments of the trail housed traps, pits filled with spikes, trip wires that triggered blades to fall from the trees like guillotine blades, and a maze of trails. To make matter worse, every fork looked identical, and with the twists and turns of the trails it was hard to tell if you were going up or down. You could easily get lost here for an eternity, never reaching the top, or even able to get back to the bottom. The reality that he may never be able to remember anything was taking its toll on his motivation to drive forward, but he was able to muster enough determination to continue on. He wouldn't let this beat him. For some reason he knew he could do it, like he had been through a lot already; he just didn't know what.

After a few more hours walking he came upon what seemed to be a lost soul. It was sitting on the ground rocking back and forth, it just stared straight forward; as if it had given up on life.

He tried to talk to it, but it took no notice. He wasn't sure how long it had been lost here, but it had already lost whatever sanity it may have had. The saddest part to this young soul was his eyes, though he only stared, he had a great fear and suffering in his eyes. The tears seemed to have carved lines thru his face; it seemed forever trapped in its own suffering.

Continuing on, he wondered if that might someday be his fate. Not knowing who, what, or why he was, or ever able to ever leave the mountain. It both terrified him and gave him reason to keep pushing forward. He had faced many traps and obstacles already, barely escaping some, but he would face a great deal many more yet if he truly desired to reach the peak.

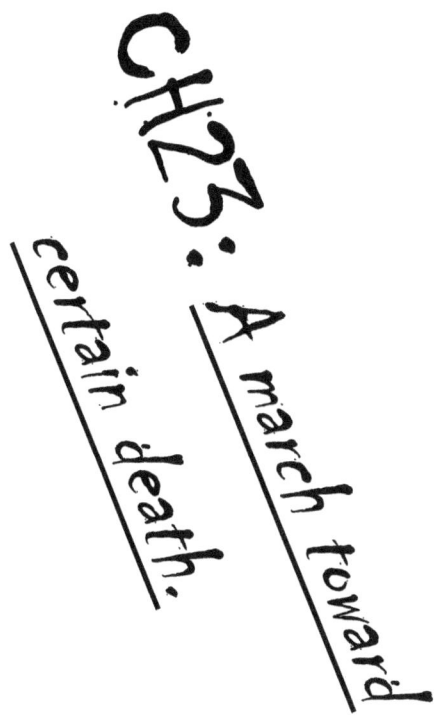

CH23: A march toward certain death.

The next day Dante and Lola set out to the crypt. They arrived just after noon. Despite searching the entire crypt and surrounding area they found nothing. Even after absolutely nothing turned up, Lola insisted that something would happen if they just waited! He reluctantly agreed, figuring a few more hours couldn't hurt. They started drawing incant marks across the walls and floors; at least if they were ambushed they would be ready. He knew they wouldn't stand a chance, but at least it seemed to ease the tension and occupy their time. They had to do something to keep their minds from wondering into the darker what-ifs that seemed to float around constantly between the two of them.

After a few more hours of waiting Dante was getting more anxious, this seemed to be more and more like a trap. He tried to convince Lola to just go back to Javax, but she would have nothing of it. Something would happen! She was so sure of it; her obsession with this idea was starting to worry Dante. Whatever amount sanity she had left was turning to desperation to find soma, defying all measurable means of logic and putting them both in danger.

A few more hours past and still nothing happened. Finally, Lola shamefully agreed to go back with him. She felt as though she was letting Soma down by leaving, but she was finally realizing that nothing was going to happen.

Just as they stood up to leave, a horrific torrent of screams outside changed the mood instantly. The kill teams were here, and there were more by the second. They both knew with the massive number of kill teams arriving they would only be able to fight for so long. Leo wouldn't be here to bail them out this time. They ran back into the crypt, and began activating all the incants they had set, fighting off the massive hordes converging on them.

No matter how many they killed, even more appeared. It was almost one long and horrible scream as the constant stream of kill teams was snapping in. the fought for hours, back to back, trying to make any progress or clear a path to escape. There was too many of them, and after hours of fighting, killing thousands of the wicked Ring minions they were running out of options. Battered and bloody, they knew exactly what their fate was going to be.

"I'm so sorry Dante.. This is my entire fault..."

"Don't blame yourself, it happens to the best of us right? Besides if this had been a trap they would've been here from the get go, it took them HOURS to show up. At least I will die in the best of company right?"

His humor helped, but they both knew it was only a matter of time before they would be completely overrun. Despite the dire situation they both fought on, until they had no fight left. They were gracefully dancing to their own demise.

Right as it appeared they were facing certain doom, John Divine appeared. Next to him was a rift into the divine plain, opening with a monstrous crackle.

"I apologize for being late my friends, but please hurry and go through the rift so I can close it behind you. As you may realize there is an army of kill teams and we haven't got much time to spare! I will have to explain this later."

Not even having time to question him at this point, they quickly crossed the rift, arriving on some outskirt of the royal palace of the ring. The rift closed right behind them. Left with no way back, or plan of action, they decided to first find somewhere out of site to stay. After all, they were now behind enemy lines. At any given moment, if they were spotted, the entire Ring army could converge on them again. Dante, having been a former resident of heaven, quickly led them to his old house. Still vacant, it was almost scary. Everything was exactly as he left it when he was drug through the streets, abducted from his wait for his brother. His looking glass, the device he used to view the mortal plain, still focused on the place his brother had lived.

Lola was taken aback by the beauty of his house. The walls seemed to glow with a golden sheen, even the dust was glowing with a golden hue. His table had been left set for two, with platinum dinnerware. Everything seemed so posh and elegant, but from stories she had been told of heaven when she was little, it wasn't so surprising. It was just amazing to her to actually be seeing it herself.

After the culture shock wore off she realized Dante seemed angrier than he had ever been. Reminded of his horrific suffering he refused to talk to Lola. He knew they would have to do something soon, but he was so overtaken by indignation that he was worried he might make a brash decision and once the Ring council got word they were in heaven, this would be the first place they would look.

They needed a plan of action. What could they do? Storm the ring palace? No, that was crazy! Or was it? If all of these kill teams were out looking for them that would leave only limited security to protect the palace. They might actually be able to pull it off; they had to do something anyway so why not try?

Dante explained his idea to Lola, expecting her to want no part of it, when, to his surprise, she leaned forward and kissed him. "That's brilliant Dante! Now let's get ready and go, while we have a chance!" He wasn't sure what to make of the kiss, but didn't have time to think of it, they needed to prepare their coup-de-grace. If they had any hope left of being able to overthrow the Ring, this was it.

CH24: To catch a sword!

Dante grabbed them each a white cloak from his closet, issuing an apology to Lola for its size. Staring at each other, they knew without saying a word what odds they faced. Either they would succeed here, or they would end up in soul prison, encased in a stone cube for the rest of eternity. The odds didn't seem to favor them, but it's the only shot they had left

They wasted no time, moving quickly across the city to the main gate of the ring palace. There were two guards stationed in front of the gate carrying gigantic swords. As they approached the gate, the guards quickly stopped them and pointed their enormous swords at Dante and Lola.

"State your business!" They roared.

Dante stepped forward, speaking casually.

"We are here for— Dolamatiz soridayd!"

The incant changed the air around the first guard into a vortex of fire. Lola simultaneously held her hand up and casting a trigon incantation, causing the other guard to become subdued in a giant triangle made of brilliant green light.

The first move had been made; they were now in even more of a race against time. They quickly proceeded further into the palace.

Surprisingly they met no other guards while searching the first corridor. As they proceeded further into the palace, every doorway seemed as though someone would jump out; but nobody did. It was almost disappointing that no one else was here. But they both knew that at least the gods would be here, somewhere.

Dante stopped Lola before they entered the throne room, asking if she still wanted to go through with this. She just leaned in, kissed him again, and nodded. She knew full well the risk they were about to take, and was ready to end this war they had started.

Dante drew a giant pentagram on the floor to use later as Lola held up her hand, and screamed at the top of her lungs:

"DESTRUCTIOP TRIGON!"

A huge triangle appeared on the door of the throne room, exploding, blasting the doors completely off.

When the smoke from the explosion cleared neither Dante nor Lola saw what they expected. In the throne room were the four chairs of the ring gods. Runa was sitting in one of them tapping her foot on the ground, a look of extreme boredom on her face. But the other three were empty. Runa reluctantly stood up, sighing, and walked toward them.

"You know, on the one hand I should be happy that you two idiots made it this easy to get rid of you, but on the other hand, did you really have to make me do this? You could've just let the kill teams catch you, would've been a lot less hassle! Here I was enjoying my peace and quiet, and you two come barging in; is that how they knock where you are from? You are so rude!"

Dante interrupted her, asking exactly what happened to the other three gods. Why she was the only one here? She told him exactly what he didn't want to hear.

"She was the only one because she was more than enough to kill the both of them, so she got stuck doing it herself."

Dante had never seen the extent of her power while working as the angel of death. He hadn't even known she was actually a god. He had figured she was just the messenger of the ring council, not one of the ring gods. But there she stood in front of them, stretching her arms, presumably getting ready to fight. On their guard Dante and Lola waited, they didn't want to make the first strike, they knew nothing of the limits of her power.

In a split second, Runa raised her left hand into the air shouting an incantation:

"Terros divinity, sabre de heavenix!"

Storm clouds began swirling over her in a hectic vortex. Dante drew a circle with his foot yelling his own incantation:

"Protectaz la moonsa!"

A wide barrier of solidified air formed across the line blocking the clouds from forming over him and Lola. But this wasn't an attack, they realized, as a golden sword descended from the vortex of clouds.

Grasping the sword Runa took off running toward Dante. Lola cast a trigon incantation:

"Restrados de majjah!"

But just as the triangle of light appeared, Runa cut through it with the sword, continuing her assault. She swung at Dante, barely missing him. He fired back with a quick flame incantation:

"demaz dragoon infiz flaris!"

A flame in the shape of a dragon formed, biting onto Runa's arm, she cut at it with her sword, the half of the dragon she cut off formed into a second dragon.

"How cute, a self-replicating fire incantation."

She casually exclaimed, taking a deep breath, and exhaling with the force of a hurricane, extinguishing the flames.

Lola tried to get an attack in from behind, firing another trigon restraint incantation, but was instantly interrupted by Runa.

"I didn't forget about you dearie!"

Runa yelled as she turned, with one slice hitting Lola across her stomach with the sword. Lola dropped to the ground, coughing up blood. Dante yelled at her in fear, not realizing just what had happened:

"What's wrong with you Lola? It's just a sword wound, your immortal, get up!"

"Not quite Dante, this sword is made from the life blood of gods. If you are not of divine nature it damages your soul on impact, and reverses immortality. Looks like I hit her just a little too hard"

Runa told him, followed by a giggle, as Lola lay on the ground, bleeding. Dante's anger began to take hold of him. He refused to let it end here; he had to get his revenge!

He kept trying to attack Runa, but no matter what he did, it seemed to have little to no effect on her. To make matters worse, constantly having to dodge her sword was quickly tiring him out.

He had one last chance. He quickly started running from the room, barely dodging, as she continued swinging the sword around. He made it to the pentagram he had drawn, lifted his left arm into the air, and shouted his Pentagramax incantation:

"Majos Pentagramxis!"

The symbol beneath him began spinning and glowing. Right as he was disappearing Runa got one good swing, lobbing Dante's arm clean off.

The pentagramax had worked, but not in time. Dante snapped into place in hell, on the giant pentagram Leo had drawn. Clutching what was left of his left arm, trying to stop the bleeding. He wasn't sure how badly his soul had been damaged by the sword. If he bled much more he would soon die. He sat on the floor trying to figure out something to do. He wondered if Lola was still alive. He needed to figure out what to do, and he needed to do it now! He was in tears from the pain and frustration he felt. He was helpless to do anything to save him or Lola.

Fighting the urge to pass out, he braced himself as a bright light appeared in the middle of the room, expanding, taking the shape of a lion's head. It let out a thunderous roar, after which its mouth began opening wider and wider until it split down the center. Runa stepped out of the lion's mouth, her Wingwave was frighteningly spectacular. Dante braced himself for the worse as she walked up to him; he was slumped against the wall, bleeding to death.

"You really are a pain Dante! You know that? Make me chase you all the way back to hell. Geez. Well Dante, got any more tricks? Have you finally given up?

No answer? Fine, then I will destroy you, you insignificant louse!"

She raised her sword, and with one powerful swing...

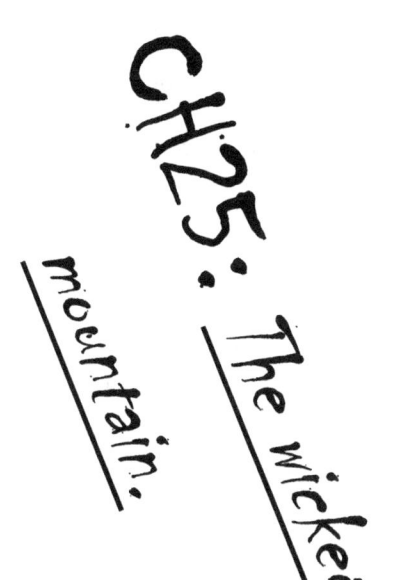

CH25: The wicked mountain.

Sitting atop the wicked mountain, having conquered the many challenges thrown upon him, the young man sat; disappointed. He still didn't remember who, what, or why he was. All the mountain had taught him was the wickedness of its tricks. He had seen lost souls with no trace of sanity, giant insects and spiders, horrific traps, designed not to kill, but to mortally wound, and leave you to die a slow death. But he had not learned anything about himself.

Sitting atop the mountain he had a pristine view of the valley below. He could even see the red gateway at the base of the mountain where he had begun. Sadly the only thing he had found at the top aside from this view was a patch of a bunch of different flowers. There was nothing else to be seen, heard, or had.

Pondering what the three voices could have possibly meant for him to find along this journey, he couldn't help but feel it may have been his fault.

"Why is everything always my fault?"

He thought to himself, wondering why those words seemed so familiar. Everything seemed so familiar to him, the wind, the words he thought, and those flowers.

But why did the flowers seem to hold such significance for him? He recognized some of them, daisies, petunias, daffodils, but wondered if these were really what they were called, or if he had made the names up. Why couldn't he remember? Whenever he tried it just seemed to make everything that much further away. He felt as though his soul was somehow broken, as if he only had fragments of it.

"..Please....we need you......"

He began hearing a voice in his head, no; it seemed to be out of thin air. Was this what it had come down to? He had lost his sanity after all? Would he spend the rest of his life here on the mountain hearing voices? Would he end up as one of the other poor souls, so tormented by his own mind that he would become a prisoner of it? No! He refused to lose his sanity. The voice continued on however, making him question if he was going crazy, or if someone was actually talking to him.

"Without you we will die........they are in trouble.....please......we need you..."

As he tried to block out the voices, failing miserably, he decided on a different approach. He yelled out to it, if they needed him so bad to show himself! The voice responded, but didn't show itself.

"You can hear me?!....John.........me here.......said......communication.....difficult...between realms..."

Just show yourself if you're real! I don't know who, what, or why I am. Can you at least tell me that much? He asked the voice, hoping for some help.

"You don't remember?....your........hope... we need ......please...."

"But I can't help you from here!"

He sighed, almost content to his fate. He must have finally gone crazy. At least he would have someone to talk to.

CH25.5: Soma's plea.

Sitting atop Mt. Majors, as John divine had told him to, he saw the ghost of Leo's spirit. John divine had told him of a theory he had for what would happen to a destroyed soul. The folklore around Mt. Majors was that the spirit of the departed past across the peak before moving on to the next realm. He only knew of the three plains of existence. Different realms of existence, dimensions of space time parallel to their own could theoretically explain how the cycle of souls worked. They would be continuously moving from one plain to the next, then to the next realm, a never ending cycle. He told Soma that if there was any hope left, he had to go to the Mountain and find a way to get Leo to cross back to this realm before he was lost forever.

The problem was, Leo's spirit didn't seem to have any recollection of what it was, and while Soma could see him, standing on the mountain, he could only seem to hear Soma. And Leo seemed to be thinking it was only a voice in his head. Soma was trying to figure out what to do next. Did that realm look the same, or different? He began to question Leo, asking him if he could see certain things. Leo answered no to most, but not all of them. It was at least somewhat similar. He could work with that.

  Soma asked Leo what he saw. "I see a valley, a red gate at the bottom, and a patch of flowers. Daisies, petunias, daffodils, and one other strange looking flower." He said they looked like something he thought he had seen before, but couldn't remember the name. Soma tried to press him to remember, but the harder he tried the further away all his memories seemed. And Leo was growing more frustrated every time Soma tried to press him to remember.

What does it look like? But Leo was getting so frustrated he just stopped answering. Staring at the valley below him, Soma kept trying to no avail. Leo's ghost was beginning to grow dimmer. If he didn't think of something soon, he might end up losing Leo forever.

CH25 3/4: Resonance.

"Why was this voice tormenting me? I told it I couldn't help, that I couldn't remember. Why won't it go away? Just let me sit in peace... "

He thought to himself, unaware the desperation of the situation.

"Please Leo......we need you...."

He didn't know who this Leo person was. Who exactly could possibly need him?! Who was even talking to him? He asked aloud, angry at his own inability to recall anything.

"Leo...Dante needs you...Lola....you..."

Why were these names so familiar? He felt like a rush of memories was about to hit him, but it was just out of his reach. He sat down, trying to clear his mind so these didn't drift away like all his other almost remembered thoughts had. Looking forward, he stared at the mystery flower. It was....black.... but what was it? The name was on the tip of his tongue...it was a....ORCHID!

It was a BLACK ORCHID! He proclaimed loudly as the world around him started to blur. He began to remember everything. Dante, Lola, Runa, it seemed to flood back all at once. As he was being drug through the gravel of time and space he felt a change in his soul. Not like when he was converted to an angel, this time it felt as though his soul itself was transcending the boundaries of mortality, his new power almost overwhelming him. Was this a god's power? The fractured remnants outlining his soul broke away, freeing its full potential. This must have been the potential Dante had seen. Perhaps with this, he could destroy Runa. No, with this he WOULD destroy Runa and put a stop to all of this once and for all!

CH26: Shattered souls.

Right as Runa's sword struck Dante, in a thunderous explosion of fire, Leo snapped into place. His presence seemed to fill the entire area, Not only was his power back, it was supercharged. Truly this new power of his was a force to be reckoned with. Runa jumped back. Fear began to fill her eyes.

"Leo, What happened to you?! Where did you get this power? I took you for a lowly angel, maybe you would make a good husband after all. What do you say? Be with me? Together we can rule all three plains of existence!"

Leo was no longer falling for her manipulative ruse. It had taken him going to the nexus plain and back to see it, losing everything about himself, to realize how stupid he had been. Ignoring Runa, he turned to Dante and asked in a completely calm voice, almost scary in its tranquility.

"Runa, Where is Lola?"

Ignoring his question, Runa lunged at him with her sword, landing a direct hit into his back.

"Don't ignore me you jerk! I asked you a question, answer me!"

She drove the sword deeper into his back.

"No answer? Fine! Then I will kill you!"

She swung the sword upward tearing open his shoulder, but he didn't bleed. Instead, flames shot out, reconnecting his skin.

Unaffected by her attack, he told her to shut up, he was busy at the moment. He didn't have time to play her little games, which only made her angrier. In her anger, she began swinging her sword, hitting him repeatedly, but he didn't even bother to dodge her attacks. Every time he was injured, flames shot out from his wounds, healing him in a mere instant.

"I told you to shut up, you wretch!"

He yelled at her, losing his patients. He held up one hand, causing her to instantly burst into flames. She began screaming from the pain, rolling around the floor trying to put them out, but they wouldn't extinguish.

"Dante, forgive my rudeness friend, but where the hell is Lola?!" He asked, as Dante lay on the ground bleeding. He didn't want to leave Dante, but he had to apologize to Lola for his stupidity.

"She was in the royal throne room; she was dying when I left Leo.... I am sorry...we underestimated Runa...how are you even here?!"

Dante struggled to speak, crying, attempting to keep enough pressure on his wounds. He knew he would soon die. "I have a pentagramax setup between here and the throne room..."

His voice getting weaker, he spoke very frankly, trying to say everything that his heart desired to speak before he passed out from the severe blood loss he had incurred.

"Go save her Leo, I just hope it's not too late..."

Speaking what appeared to be his last words; Leo felt pity for his friend, his savior so many years ago. But now, he was left powerless to help his friend, he did not possess the power to raise the dead.

Leo left using the pentagramax. Upon his arrival in the throne room of heaven, he was met with a heartbreaking scene. On the floor, in a pool of her own blood, was Lola. Her hand outstretched, she had written a message using her blood. "Don't forget me." And a sad face drawn next to it ":(". Indeed, he would not forget about her, because he had loved her. It had just taken him far too long to see it.

His anger reaching a point of hellish fury, he used the pentagramax to return to hell. In a fit of rage he picked up Runa, who had just managed to extinguish the flames, slamming her into the wall. "Today you die wretch!" He yelled at her, with a ferocious vigor echoing from his voice. He put his other hand over her face, and asked if she had any last words.

"Killing me won't bring her back Leo. I just-"

In an instant, without a spoken word, flames engulfed her once more. This time she had no escape, he held her in place until she had been burned to ash. She had died, but he was left disappointed. He had expected his vengeance to be fulfilling, but this did nothing for the aching in his heart. It was almost driving him to a point of madness, it hurt so badly but nothing he did could make it stop.

The god of death had achieved his victory over the corrupted ring god, Runa, but at what price? He had to give up everything. The only friends he had gained were now dead. The woman he loved had died before he could even tell her how he felt. His heart was weighing down on him, broken clean in two.

Tears rolling down his face, he wondered what would come next for the world he had saved, and the angels were now free of Runa and her oppression. He was now left the ruler of all three plains. Dante's dream had been realized, but Dante had died before seeing it. Everything had been for nothing! Having no one to share this victory with, Leo screamed in his anguish; but no one was there to hear him.

CH27 : Troubling news.

This is quite troubling said one voice in the darkness, very troubling agreed a second voice, most urgently troubling replied a third voice. I fear we may need to break some rules to fix this problem, said the first voice. Finally coming around then eh, replied the third voice. We must not break the rules we have set Said the second voice; It could upset the balance of the world! You saw what happened when we broke the rules with Runa!

Or perhaps sometimes we must break the rules, to undo the damage caused by breaking the rules, reasoned the first voice. Perhaps, agreed the third. Possibly, the second voice hesitantly agreed.

But how shall we fix this storm we have unleashed upon our realm? Even by breaking the rules it will be difficult to stop the monster we have created, Said the second voice. Perhaps there is only one way; we must bring back that which was lost, the third said.

L&D The Chronicles of Life and Death.

But that which is lost now belongs to the next realm,
we have already angered the controllers of that realm
by our last deeds. How do you propose we do this?
That we still need to figure out, hopefully in time it
will become clear. The first two agreed.

Until then we shall have to send everything we have to
buy more time, and hope we are not too late.

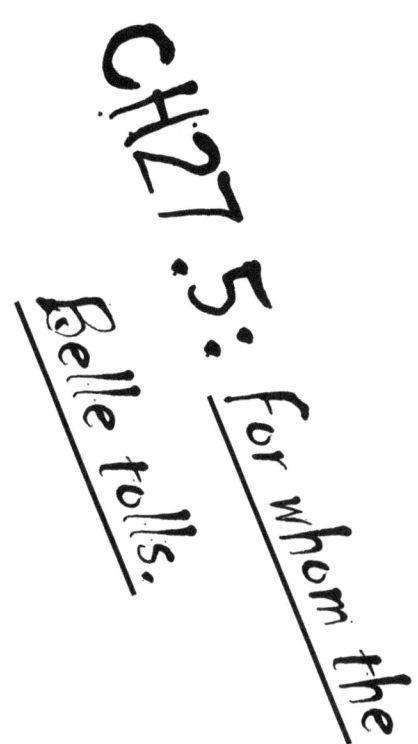

CH27.5: For whom the Belle tolls.

"In the end I have nobody, in the end nobody shall remain!" Leo mused to himself as he walked from the royal palace of the heavens. He had spent the last 10 hours setting up for his finale. "Grand majos DESTRUCTIOP OMNI SULAS!" In the distance throughout the entire angelic plain, an odd whistle was heard. The whistle then turned into a hum, which turned into a buzz, which turned into a massive explosion. The explosion was seen and heard across the heavens. It was a grand introduction as Leo began his rampage, destroying the palace.

As soon as the explosion was seen, the familiar torrent of screams bombarded him as the kill teams snapped into place, immediately followed by the sound of an incredibly powerful bell.

"Leo, you must stop this, before you destroy everyone!"

A very tall man began speaking, walking up through the seemingly endless swarm of kill teams. They bowed to him as he walked past them. And he had such a familiar voice; it was one of the voices he had heard in the darkness. The man stood a towering 7 feet, towering over the kill teams. His eyes and face reflected his long life. His hair was long since grayed, but well groomed. His demeanor reflected his stature; he beamed of importance and power.

"We did not return you to this plain, against the wishes of the nexus gods, to destroy our realm! If you do not stop, I, Gabrielle the holy Belle will destroy you where you stand! You have freed us to return to this realm by killing Runa, but do not mistake that for a debt. We will protect the souls of our realm at any cost!"

"You did this? You brought me back here? You sent me up the mountain?! If you had just told me who I was, I could have saved them. IF YOU HAD JUST TOLD ME, I WOULD HAVE SAVED THEM! WHY?

WHY WAS THAT SO DIFFICULT??!!" Leo's voice was filled with an unholy rage, his anger overtaking his sense of reason.

"I will not be stopped, Gabrielle of the holy belle, I will destroy your entire realm in payment for the loss of my loved ones. I WILL BURN ALL OF IT TO OBLIVION!!"

"If you refuse reason, then you will force my hand Leo. I will ask you once more, stop this at once!"

Gabrielle replied, staring at Leo with the years of his wisdom reflecting from his eyes, hoping he would somehow return reason to the monster in front of him.

No such luck, Leo raised a hand toward him, fire forming around it, Gabrielle had no choice now, he had to act immediately.

"Refutes le abridge of belle!"

He yelled while raising both hands. All that could be heard was the sound of a bell, repeatedly being struck; it seemed to distort space itself.

Leo was knocked off balance as the bell continued to ring, he couldn't even see straight. It was like looking through a mirage.

As he tried to regain his bearing, Gabrielle walked forward, striking him to the ground.

"Leo, stop this! I don't want to destroy you."

"Yes, but I do want to kill you!"

Leo screamed back at him, attempting to climb back to his feet, before being struck down again.

"Leo, why must this continue? You cannot even stand up, just stop!"

But Leo would not; he once again was attempting to get to his feet.

"You wouldn't understand you old relic! I LOST THEM! ALL OF THEM!"

Screaming, he was fighting against the distortion around him.

"Then forgive me Leo, but I must end this."

He raised one arm up, grabbing Leo with the other.

"Immaculate thunderstrus of bellegret-"

But before he could Finnish, Leo grabbed his arm, and with unholy speed he yelled: "grandos ingicio!" Gabrielle's arm instantly burst into black flames. The sound of the bell ceased, Gabrielle knew what this was, the un-extinguishable flames of hell. With the confidence and cool mindedness only a god could possess, he quickly ripped it off, saving himself.

"Leonardo Leon, this is not acceptable, I retreat for now, but expect my return. We will not tolerate your destruction of our realm!"

In the sound of the bell being struck twice, he was gone. The kill teams, that had been standing clear before, began to close in on Leo.

"You will die too, servants of the gods!"

Raising his hand, he screamed an incantation.

"majos grande ignicios!"

A swirl of black flames began rising around him, the spinning vortex growing larger, until it encompassed all that stood before him. As the vortex disappeared, every member of the kill teams before him lay in various stages of being burned to death. One of the men that lay dying, burning in black flames, reached out, pleading to Leo.

"Please, at least tell my wife and kids I loved them. I..."

"Don't worry; for soon they too will be burned from existence, you insignificant whelp!"

What was left of his humanity had died with Lola. "You're a monster!" Screamed the dying man, tears rolling down his face, he couldn't seem to comprehend this inhumanity, he was just doing his job; and now him, and his family were going to die.

Leo continued to burn the divine plain, ignoring the cries for mercy, no man woman or child was spared. Inside he had stopped caring, the only purpose he had left was to share his pain with everyone around him. He would provide the world with the same intense pain he now felt; the world would know his wrath.

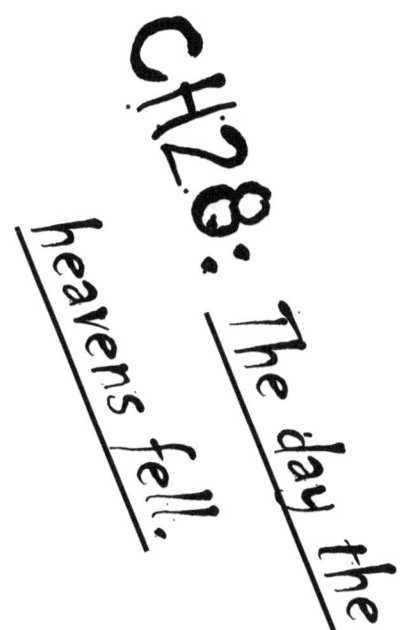

CH28: The day the heavens fell.

"Oh dear, this might be an issue!"

Declared one of the three voices in the darkness.

"Dear me, he seems to have made off with your arm!"

"I am fine; shall we focus on the main matter at hand?"

Said another voice, in frustration.

"He will not stop, reason has left him."

Continued the voice, the sorrow overtaking his frustration.

"Now we must destroy him Gabrielle."

"But it will not be that simple Micheal!"

"I will make it that simple!"

Micheal yelled back, his emotions clearly presenting the urgency of the situation.

"Don't underestimate him Micheal that has already cost me an arm!"

The destruction of the divine plain continued, innocent souls, the very same Leo had fought so valiantly to free from Runa, now lost forever. As Leo continued his rampage, he ended up near the soul prison.

Memories of rescuing Lola and Dante rushed back into his mind, only angering him further. As he began chanting his incants, summoning dark flames of hell, a familiar voice spoke to him, crying.

"Hey mister, why are you destroying our homes? Did we somehow hurt you? Please don't kill my family..."

The young boy, who had helped him enter the prison safely, was standing before him.

Without as much as a shred of remorse, Leo cast the black flames of hell. He lit the little boy and his family on fire with the unholy flames of hell.

"I thought you were a hero mister! You're a monster!"

The little boy screamed at him, as his body burned, yet another casualty of the monster currently devouring the heavens with the black flames of hell. He was just another victim of Leo's wrath.

As his rampage continued to devour the heavens, leaving only ash scattered across the plain, he approached a giant pillar of light. The scale and beauty of it was incomprehensible. The pillar reached from the sky to the ground, seeming to support the heavens themselves.

On his approach toward the towering pillar, the outline of a gate began to appear from the light. It quickly swung open with a large groan, revealing a tall slender man, with a halo of light above his head. This mysterious man stood 7ft tall and he held a giant spear in his hand. The handle was made of gold and steel with ornate emerald designs. The blade was encrusted in diamonds.

"Leo, I Micheal, gatekeeper of the divine plane, will stop you. If you advance any further, I will kill you!"

The air of confidence was not only clear in his voice; it was in a league of its own. It was clear, concise, and powerful.

Leo began to walk toward him, completely un-phased by the threats made against his life. Micheal took notice and wasted no time taking up a fighting stance, raising his spear high above his head.

"Gran gotis re amora dozem!"

At the sound of his voice twelve enormous gates began to form around them, titanic in size, enclosing them in from all directions. They were formed from the light itself; leaving only a shadow where the light had been.

With the stage now set, Micheal began his assault. He mercilessly started swinging at Leo. His blows were powerful and accurate. Leo managed to dodge the first blow, but the subsequent hits began slicing him up, he couldn't even get an incantation finished between the hits.

With one final stab, it appeared the fight had drawn to a close; Leo was impaled through his heart. Micheal then drove the spear into the ground, effectively trapping Leo in place.

"Segratis mu tol leis!"

At his command, all the gates surrounding them opened. It unleashed a massive swarm of golden bugs. The bugs began to cover Leo, swarming him, until he was completely covered by them. Leo's life seemed to be over, but that assumption was soon broken. It was with a massive blast that Micheal realized how much harder this fight would be.

"I am afraid someone already broke my heart Micheal! However I will be more than happy to obliterate you as well, you pest of a god!"

The words rang through the air as a massive blast of black flames began pouring out, the black flames of hell, burning the golden bugs surrounding him. When Leo emerged, the toll on his body was evident. His tears flowing from his eyes, it was plain as day exactly how far he had come; he cried the black flames of hell. His pain was now his only purpose; he had nothing else left except for his sorrow. He pulled out the spear, screaming from the intense pain. He would have his retribution; he threw the spear to the ground, struggling to regain his upright footing.

Micheal quickly grabbed his spear and began another bloody onslaught, landing hit after hit, stabbing into the battered body that Leo remained in.

His pain was still driving him, but his body had seemed to reach its limit.

"Just a little more, I just need a little more time!"

He thought to himself, fighting the intense pain shooting through his body, as Micheal continued destroying his body with an unholy ferocity.

But, as he was, all the time in the world wouldn't have helped him. He realized this as he was again impaled; this time to the wall. Struggling to break himself free, his strength began failing him. His body had long since passed its breaking point from the assault.

"I refuse to stop, damn you Micheal, DAMN YOU!"

He screamed, his rage boiling to the surface, fueled by his helplessness.

"I WILL NOT STOP!!"

The black flames of hell began engulfing him, burning away the outer shell of his humanity; what was left anyway. His darkened soul began to grow, the black flames took the shape of a giant, two headed, canine. The vessel of his soul now encased not in flesh, but in the burning black flames of hell. He had become a beast.

Micheal was too slow, with a burst of hellish speed, unlike anything he had ever seen before, Leo tore into Micheal. The bite left a flaming gape in Micheal's left arm.

This new form was something even Micheal had been unprepared for. It moved with unmatchable speed and his eyes couldn't even seem to keep up with it. HE tried unsuccessfully, to dodge the rabid bites from both heads, but was hopelessly outmatched

With one last bite to the throat, Micheal was no more. His fate, the one he had chosen, led him to fall with the divine plain, his kingdom.

CH.29: Chaos.

As the hell-beast, Leo, destroyed the pillar of light that held the heavens in place, the entire divine plane crashed down into the mortal plain. If ever there was an end of the world, this had to be it. The fallout immediately following was immense; billowing into the distance. Chaos began to break out over the entire mortal plain, massive amounts of death, destruction, and fear had sent the population into a panic.

They tried to fight the hell-beast, but nothing the mortals had could affect him. The nations of their world sent army's; they tried everything they had to no avail.

"We cannot wait any longer Ishmael; we have to do it now! Micheal was the strongest of us and he has died! Screw the nexus gods wishes, if we do not encroach on them for this, we will have no realm to exist in!"

"Very well Gabrielle, I will open the way between realms, but it will take every ounce of my strength to do it, I only hope it is not too late brother. And beyond all else, survive!"

The sound of a mighty horn bellowed and light burst through the darkness.

A wounded Gabrielle reluctantly watched his brother summon every last ounce of strength he had to open the rift between the realms. It was quiet a site regardless of the circumstances; Ishmael was a towering 8ft. tall. He had a white wing on his left shoulder and a white one on his right. He held a golden horn high into the air, adorned with ruby and sapphire, sounding off with a holy cadence of melody. Even the air around him began to tear apart, separating like a curtain. Behind it was revealed, the nexus realm.

"Goodbye brother"

Gabrielle said, with tears in his voice, as he crossed to the nexus realm. Looking back he saw only his brother Ishmael, fading into the distance, as he used every last drop of energy his soul had to make sure there realm could survive. Struggling to choke back the sorrow he felt for his brother, he hoped it would not be in vain.

The residents of the nexus realm were not expecting his visit. As the rift was opened between realms and the one armed god emerged through it they began to scream and run in fear.

Having caused such a commotion, his presence was instantly recognized by the Nexus gods. Three clouds fell from the sky. As the hit they assumed a humanoid form, swords drawn, they addressed Gabrielle.

"What treachery is this Ringling? You dare encroach into our realm?! Again?! This is an act of war you scum!" Their voice was coarse and rough, booming from the cloud doubles."

"I had no choice—"

"There is always a choice Ringling!"

Before he could even respond, all 3 swords had been forced through his heart.

His vision began fading, the last thoughts he had were only questions. What had they done wrong?

They had tried to be fair and just gods. They protected the mortal souls in their realm. They had cared only for the well-being of those they protected. It wasn't their fault that Runa had betrayed them and sealed them away.

But, in a revelation that came far too late, he realized it was their fault. If they had never sent Leo back in the first place, the realm wouldn't be in ruins. They may have remained sealed, but the realm would have survived. Leo had freed them by passing over, breaking the incant that had sealed them away. The desire for revenge against Runa had been their downfall. They were responsible for the monstrosity unleashed. They had turned him from the hero he was, into a vessel for revenge. They had corrupted him on the most basic level.

His breathing becoming strained, he knew his time was short. Tears running from his eyes he cried, not over the loss of himself, but of the many souls he had been protecting for so long; over his brothers, over his own corruption. But there was truly no one left to care, nobody left to tell him it wasn't his fault. Nobody would even remember them or their realm.

In a matter of minutes the ring gods had become extinct. Dante, Lola, and Leo had their revenge; however twisted it may have turned out to be.

CH30: Song of sorrows.

As the rest of the ring realm was destroyed by the Hell-beast, another struggle was silently fighting to stop the madness; to stop the rampaging beast.

Leo was broken inside; his heart had split in two. His mind filled with anger but inside a small sliver of humanity was left. The only clue that it even existed was the stream of tears and the sorrow in the roar of the beast. He was a prisoner of his own rage and remorse.

He continued to destroy the ring realm until there was nothing left. But after he had obliterated everything he was left sad and alone with nothing to comfort him but black flames and his sorrow.

He began to howl an unholy song. It was filled with sorrow, with the weight of his pain. The bitterness of his revenge was biting back at him; he had killed everyone. Innocent or guilty, it had made no difference to him. The howl became even sadder as time carried on, louder, as if he was seeking a reply.

As the sad song continued, a soft voice, almost unheard, caused the beast to spin around searching for its source with a maddening desperation.

"Oh Leo, what have you done now?"

Standing in the middle of the flames, was Lola. Tears rolling down her face, staring at what used to be the man she loved, she was heartbroken and scared. As sorrow continued to flow from her eyes, she stood, trembling, the beast before her was no longer Leo. Somewhere deep inside she knew there had to be some trace of him, but he was so far gone that it would take a miracle. Regardless of the odds she knew she had to at least try to get through to whatever was left of him.

"Please Leo, please, just come back to me. I LOVE YOU!"

The words seemed to be reaching him, or so she thought, as the flames began subsiding. The howl turned into a sob of regret; the ballad of a broken soul. When the last of the flames went out all that was left was a tired and lonely man, sobbing on the ground.

"What have I done?! WHAT HAVE I DONE?!"

He cast his head into his hands, the tears collecting around him; he was not even able to look Lola in the eye. He had destroyed everything, and everyone they had fought so hard to protect, to save. He had gone from almighty hero, to the greatest evil they had ever seen. He had murdered everyone in cold blood.

"Lola, I never got to tell you, I'm such a fool. Please forgive me...But...I killed them...all of them. I destroyed everything. I have become the very monster we fought to stop, no, I've become worse. But I did it all for you..."

He threw his head back into his hands as his tears could no longer be held back.

Lola walked over to him. Reaching out, she put her forehead against his, speaking in a soft voice and choking back her own tears as much as possible.

"Leo, why would you think I wanted this? I love you, I really do, but I can't forgive you for this. You killed everyone! You destroyed everything! My heart wants to forgive you, but I can't. You've truly become a monster Leo; A heartless beast.

I love you for who you were, but I hate you for what you've become!"

He pushed her away, the rejection causing a horrific pain in the depths of his soul, burning away at his heart.

"I can't fix this Lola..."

Holding one hand to the heavens he screamed out an incantation beyond that of the highest order, a voice so majestic it was awe inspiring.

"Gran majos del RI awe mus re homla!"

Moving his hand down, parallel to the ground and pointing at Lola, a grand light began to engulf her.

"Forgive me Lola."

He cast one last somber look to her before averting his gaze.

"Goodbye Lola..."

In a brilliant flash of light the world began spinning around her, time and space began to lose, and regain shape, in an ever recurring cycle. The sensation of flying and falling were both overtaking her at the same time. It felt like a dream like a dream. As her head started spinning, she realized she was about to black out. She tried to hold her composure, but everything slowly faded to black.

CH31: John Divines Intervention.

Blurred vision, she tried to stand up, losing her balance. Her memory seemed fuzzy, but was starting to return in small chunks.

She screamed for Leo, but he was nowhere to be found. Where was she? This landscape seemed so familiar, and it was. This is where she had ended up after she died. This was the nexus plain?! Had Leo killed her? Why couldn't she remember? What had happened to her? Her thoughts starting to overwhelm her, she had to stop and think, figure out what was going on.

After calming herself down, as much as she could at least, with the current circumstances, she began looking around; trying to make sure she knew where she was.

The landscape was that of a city on the edge of a forest. The beauty of the natural landscape seemed to compliment the futuristic styling of the buildings.

She seemed to be in the outskirts of the city, directly on the edge of the forest. Shadows cast from the trees made it almost a surreal scene, seeming to paint the sides of the buildings with the darkness that surrounded the entire city.

"Am I dead?" She mused aloud to herself, as if the answer might jump out to her, almost laughing at her own stupidity. But, to her surprise, it did. In a brilliant flash of light, a familiar strange little man appeared right before her very eyes.

"I am afraid you not quite dead my dear! You are in fact, quite alive. I apologize if I have burst your bubble my dear friend, but I still require some help."

It was such a familiar voice; she turned to see John Divine. Well, it wasn't really him, but a half transparent image of him. It was almost like staring at a ghost. She wanted to ask him exactly how he was managing to do this, but she really didn't have time.

He continued speaking so fast that he rarely even had enough time between sentences to take a breath.

"I hope you can forgive me, I had to send you back to that realm to stop him from destroying the limbo between our realms. If he had managed to destroy it, I would have died as well. Don't tell the nexus gods please; they get so angry at just the smallest things! But, I digress, back on the topic of things precluding to you, that you would actually care about in any amount of measurable emotions,

I had to restore your soul to a pre-death state. I do apologize for the painful memories, would you like me to put your soul back to the clean slate it has been recently, like your death did?"

She was quick to interrupt him at this point to establish the fact that she did NOT want to die again. Stating curtly, and quickly:

"No. Thank you Mr. Divine, but I think I would rather keep the memories of my love, of what he used to be. What I would like however, is to know exactly how I got here! If I didn't die, what happened? What exactly is going on?"

"I believe Leo used an Echelon class incantation to send you here. Though I really have no way to be certain, I have never actually seen one before. They are supposed to be an impossible incantation; I have only ever heard legends of them. Supposedly, they use the very life force of a soul combined with some unknown factor. But that's about all I know about them. No one has ever been near an entity powerful enough to use them, not anybody that has survived anyway."

Without any for warning his image began to flicker, and distort. It was almost like watching a reflection passing through an entire set of funhouse mirrors. It began wildly going from large to small and every size and shape in between.

Oopsy, looks like we will have to continue this conversation later, I need to recharge my energy. This cross realm projection really takes a lot! It's a major pain trying to cross stabilize the interval cortex pre- "

In a matter of a second, his image disappeared. She was left with far more questions than answers, but it did seem to be his calling card. She was remembering things a little better now, the details slightly back to mind, she was far from actually being able to piece together the entire happenings that had recently transpired. She was really trying though and had managed to figure out a baseline of the events.

John Divine had somehow, without the nexus gods realizing, snuck her soul back to the ring realm, and restored her memories from her past life. He had used a desperate measure for his self-preservation. He had succeeded where the ring gods had failed, barely. He had been the only survivor of the realm, aside from herself, well she didn't think she was there, but it was hard to tell at this point with her lack of clear memories.

She kept trying to force out more detail, mulling over everything as many times as she could. Her thoughts were cut short however, as a team of men wearing all black uniforms, with a white circle on the front, began materializing from the shadows. In a mere matter of seconds she was surrounded from all directions. Before she could even raise her hand to cast an incantation, she felt a sudden, sharp stinging sensation on her shoulder, had one of them shot her with something?

She didn't know what was going on; her mind raced trying to figure it out. Her arms weren't working, and her legs seemed to be doing the opposite of what she was willing them to do. Nothing made sense to her right now, everything started happening so fast, and her world seemed to spin around her. Everything seemed like a dream to her at this point, as they knocked her down, and bound her hands with some weird foam substance. It seemed to solidify, almost instantly, into a stone like material. They then proceeded to blindfold, and gag her. It was like watching a nightmare, she was helpless. She couldn't even make herself scream.

She was terrified as to what they would do to her, but she had no recourse to even struggle. Still dazed, she could barely keep up with all the voices around her, where they picking her up? Where were they taking her? Why didn't they talk to her? She felt as if she was just an object from the way they were treating her. When she tried to squeeze a muffle past the gag, but again nothing would come out. Was her mouth even moving? She was trying so hard to struggle, but her body was motionless as they carried it away. The only thing her body seemed to agree with her on at the moment was her tears; they left a trail as she was being abducted.

Somewhere in the distance she heard a horrific sound, like metal being ripped in half. The men carrying her body seemed to notice too. They began yelling and shouting about how they needed to hurry, before "He" got here.

They seemed to be moving toward the city, the lights flashing by, almost hypnotic in the steady flow. They must have been moving pretty fast. After a while, they must have passed into a different part of the city, it seemed to be getting darker. Wherever they were taking her, was in the thicket of buildings toward the core of the city. The tall buildings surrounding them cast down the ominous shadows on the street, choking out whatever natural light attempted to reach the streets.

An explosion somewhere in the backdrop of the city momentarily aroused her senses. She wondered who, or what, was causing such a commotion. But, what she really wanted to know was why this happening to her, who these men that had abducted her were, and what they had shot her with that had her so knocked out?

Another explosion rang through the streets, was it closer? It may have been. She couldn't keep her focus, everything was starting to fade, and it was getting so dark.

CH32: Scream.

Darkness, all she could see was the darkness around her. It was cold, damp, and eerily quiet. All she remembered was the last few sounds until she passed out. The blindfold and gag was gone, and her hands were free, but she didn't want to be here, it was horrifying. An even worse thought crossed her mind, what would happen when she left here? As far as she could reason, her immortality would not apply in this realm. She would be a mere mortal here. Well, a mere mortal who knew how to incant.

"Please let me out of here...it's so dark... PLEASE!" She screamed, pleaded, begged, and sobbed for hours. Either nobody was there, or they just didn't care. Was she even still alive? Her hopelessness was setting in, a strong pain in her heart, why was this happening? What had she done to deserve this? Every tear burned as it rolled down her face, falling to the ground, with the thousands of other tears, forming a puddle around her.

As time rolled along it never got any easier. Crying until she fell asleep, and then crying more.

She was trying to hold it together, but she couldn't. She felt like she was losing her mind. She had no way to know how much time had passed, an hour? 3 days? It felt like a year had already past. The uncertainty of her future was wearing down all her nerves. She wondered how much longer she could even cry, before she ran out of tears; they didn't even give her food or water. Her hunger was causing sharp pains through her stomach. The thirst made it seem like a large wad of cotton was stuffed in her mouth.

At this point there was little doubt about it; she had been left here to die. And no one would even remember her, except maybe John Divine. That jerk, this was mostly his fault. She wanted to be able to blame him, to be able to blame someone, but she knew in his place she would have probably done the same thing.

As she faced thoughts of her newfound mortality she knew there was most likely a different realm her soul would pass on to, but she would lose every essence of her being. It might as well just be someone else's soul after that.

She wondered who she had been in this realm, what she had thought before her soul was reverted. Had she been a good person? Maybe a little bit of a bitch? Had she done something so horrific that they had turned a blind eye to her disappearance, or had John Divine truly been able to sneak her soul out without the nexus gods realizing anything had happened at all?

Even though it was her own soul, she almost felt like someone else had died just for her to exist. It didn't matter now anyway, the aching hunger and dying thirst were just getting worse, and she wasn't sure how much longer she would remain as herself, or among the living.

Going through the room twice, she found all the walls, but no door. Figuring they must have dropped her in from the ceiling or it was some sort of pit. Trying to find a way to climb the walls, they were too smooth, a polished form of marble. She tried hitting them with her fists, it only caused pain. The walls strength far outweighed that of her. She tried to use incantations, but none seemed to work, was it the realm? Or whatever they had injected her with? Or was it just not possible in this realm?

Her head ached from the screaming and crying, fists throbbing from the attempts to break through the wall. Curling up in a ball in the corner head between her knees, she rocked back and forth. What would happen when she died? Would it be painless? Would it hurt? She didn't remember anything from before. As far as she could tell, she had ceased to exist after her last death. Her soul had moved on, but it had been someone completely different. The thought of completely being wiped from existence pried more tears and another bout of self-pity and sobbing.

Desperate for something, anything to keep herself from dying she began to screaming again, screaming a thousand times, not even a scurry from a bug, she was truly left completely alone. She was near death, trying so hard to remain conscious. Her will to go on was fading as her body succumbed to the dehydration, hunger, and fatigue. Before she knew it, the dark seemed to be fading into a light. She could see a bright light in the distance; it seemed to beckon for her. Could this be her death? Was this what happened to her consciousness? She refused to walk into her own death.

But as much as she tried to resist, her body seemed to move on its own. Rising to its feet, walking toward the light, she screamed at herself to stop! But nothing she did seemed to affect it. She was marching to her own demise, and was powerless to stop it. This couldn't be happening, not to her, she refused to let it. She would do anything, ANYTHING!

"Why do you fight so hard young one? Why do you not accept your fate, just move on to the next realm?"

It was such an odd voice, both soothing, and sinister at the same time. Resisting her first instincts to trust it and follow its suggestion, she managed to force out a reply:

"Because, I have to find Leo, I can't die, not without seeing him at least one more time. Regardless of what he has become, or done, I still love him!"

"Then you know what you must do, don't you? You must stop yourself from crossing over, at any cost. Are you willing to risk your humanity on that? Are you willing to transcend your soul's limitations? Are you willing to give up your humanity? If you remove the shell constraining your soul and die, there would be nothing left to pass on. That shell is all that protects it, what transports it safely to the next realm. Would you risk the entire essence of your being, just to see him? Is it worth that much to you?"

But he didn't have to wait for her answer, she jabbed her own hand into her stomach, felt what seemed to be her heart, no, this must be her soul. Instinctively she began squeezing it with every last ounce of strength she had left, fighting through the excruciating pain; she was trying to crush the shell encasing it. The pain mounted higher, the room getting dark again. She couldn't seem to do it, but she had too. She had to do this! She refused to give up. She imagined Leo's face, mustering one last burst of strength, screaming, the shell crushed in her hand, unleashing a huge surge of energy through her body. She began losing control; her energy was overflowing out of her body, despite her best efforts to control it. She collapsed to the floor as a blast of green energy expelled itself from her.

CH33: Of angels and beasts.

Angels:

As she rose from the floor, two enormous green wings unfurled from her back, a brilliant, blazing green in color. A triangular green halo formed over her head, the same brilliant glow emanating from it. Over each hand a green triangle floated, like a hologram. Was this the true form of her soul, when all the limitations had been removed?

Looking up, the room illuminated by the blazing glow of her wings and halo, she saw a hatch, on the ceiling. With one upward bound, she crashed through it, reaching freedom. Flying high into the sky, she saw how badly the realm had been ravaged by destruction.

Who had done this? She wondered, surveying the destruction. Entire buildings were destroyed, reduced to smoldering rubble. Bodies were scattered across the ground. Then, in a single moment she knew without a doubt exactly who had done this, she saw a single black flame burning. Leo had been here. He was going to destroy this realm just like he had done to theirs.

Searching for some clue as to where he was, it seemed this destruction had happened quite some time ago. But, by following trail of destruction it would lead right to him. There was so much that it was hard to tell which direction she needed to go, but after a larger survey of her surroundings the trail became clear.

Beasts:

After he sent Lola to the nexus realm, Leo was at an end. Should he just let her be? Let her live in nexus, never to see him again?

Her rejection was still fresh in his mind, his heart aching from the venom in her words, but he couldn't just leave her. As much as he longed for her happiness, he longed for her companionship more. His selfishness was killing him, he wanted to let her go, but he couldn't. He just couldn't let her walk away. He had made a mistake sending her away, he needed to make things right, to fix this mess he had created. His only option now was to go to nexus and try to win her back, but could he do it? Or was this just a lost cause? It didn't matter, the only fight lost is the fight never fought, he thought to himself.

 With a grand scream and a great effort he tore a rift between the realms, just long enough to slip through. He wasn't entirely sure how he suddenly knew how to do all these things, but he didn't mind the power that was now at his disposal. It was like a drug to him, the more he used it, and the more he wanted to test the limits of them.

At once, responding to the thunderous crash on the nexus side, from the rift forming, the cloudian forms of the nexus gods appeared before him. They drew their swords, they were out for blood. They would not even be interested in talking to this new intruder in the realm.

"Out of my way, I have no business with you!" Leo snapped at them, ignoring the grand blades pointed at him, ready to take his blood, his very soul.

"You do know Ringling, trespassing into nexus is forbidden. As such, we will destroy you, the same as the last visitors, the ring gods! And that girl that recently crossed here from your realm.."

"WHAT DID YOU JUST SAY?" His demeanor changed in an instant. The rage built up inside him like a hot ember starting to blaze. "IF YOU LAYER ONE FINGER ON HER.."

"It's too late for her, she is gone." They snidely replied in unison.

He was silent as the news sunk in. He had sent her here, He was the only reason she ended up here, and now she was dead? *No. NO!* This couldn't be! There had to be a mistake.

He was silent, as a statue, trying to comprehend what he had done, what had happened.

But the silence was quickly broken as a sword plunged through his chest, the pain radiating across his entire body. His blood was no longer golden, it was red, as a mortals?! What was happening? How was this possible? He was a god, or so he thought. But he was bleeding red, as a mere mortal would.

"Your just as much of a fool as the ring god, did you really think your divine status, or your immortality would apply here? Guess again Ringling. You are just a mortal here, and your soul will be destroyed, you removed the shell protecting it already. Do you have any last words before your soul ceases to exist?"

His words were cold and serious, he was not kidding either, and the situation was quickly getting very dire.

The hot flow of blood flowing from his chest, served as yet another reminder that if he didn't do something soon, he would die, as a mortal.

His mind was becoming a blur; the blood loss was starting to severely affect his ability to think. He strained to gain his bearing, but his concentration kept falling back to his own helplessness, it was like he was back to that night hiding behind the bushes; he had come too far to stop now.

"Will you truly say nothing? YOU ARE PATHETIC!"

Another sword drove through his stomach, and the third through his back, the pain overwhelming any sense of reason he had left. He collapsed to the ground, writhing in pain.

How could this be possible? This couldn't be happening, it had to be some sort of a dream, and he couldn't die, not here! He was determined to fight through the pain, to survive, no matter what it took.

"If you have nothing to say, then we will end you here Ringling. You are an insignificant whelp in our world, and you will not be forgiven for your insolence! "

"STOP! JUST STOP! I WILL NOT BE KILLED NOT BY YOU!"

Black flames began pouring out of his wounds once again; it was his blood itself burning. Engulfing his entire body, the flames once more took the form of a double headed canine. When the flames took their final form, the mighty beast let out a thunderous howl. The destruction would continue.

In an instant he destroyed the cloud doubles used by the nexus gods, as if they were nothing but ragdolls. Afterwards, he made short work of any surrounding structure, completely annihilating everything that had the unfortunate luck of being near him.

The sound of metal being ripped was heard across the plain as he rampaged, his broken heart once again blinding him, he wanted nothing more than their blood, as payment for hurting her. He was once again out for blood, he didn't care the overall after effect or cost, he just wanted to kill them all for what they had done.

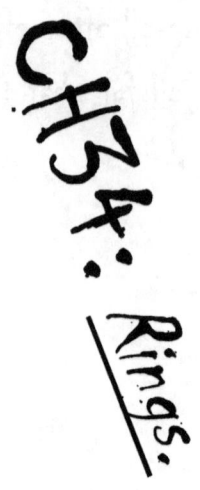

CH34: Rings.

Soaring across the sky, still searching for Leo, following the destruction, she saw a pillar of flames shoot toward the atmosphere on the horizon. This had to be Leo, but why was he out of control again? She needed to stop him before he destroyed this realm too.

The scene was almost surreal, he had destroyed everything he came upon, leaving little more than ash in his wake. She was prepared to do whatever it took to stop him this time, whatever it took.

Flying toward the pillar, she saw what she was hoping had not happened. Leo had once again lost his humanity, turning into the giant flaming canine. Bodies lie, strewn as far as the eye could see. Burned, beaten, and shredded, they had been murdered in cold blood. There were three men, wearing golden robes with golden swords, attempting to hold the beast at bay; he actual Nexus gods.

They were not, however, winning. There fatigue was showing as they got flipped around. The hell beast whipping his two heads, tail furiously. It finally managed to pin one down, spitting hellishly dark flames over him. Despite the best efforts of the other two gods to save him, a blood curdling scream was heard, bones being crushed, the sound of a god being killed.

In the blink of an eye, another of the men was caught in the jaws, split clean in half. The other launching one final, desperate assault, caught off guard as the tail swung around toward his face; knocking him to the ground. He braced himself for death as a gigantic paw came crashing down. He closed his eyes, cringing, hoping against all odds that somehow something would save him.

But death did not come for him; a giant emerald trigon pushed away the paw, throwing the beast off balance; and another, pinning the beast to the ground.

The brilliance of the figure before him was almost blinding. Her magnificent emerald wings, the triangular halo, she was truly the form befitting of a goddess. And her strength was well apparent from the massive amount of energy radiating from her body.

She wasted no time as the beast rose again, she cast out another emerald trigon with her other hand, using both she quickly pinned the beast back to the ground. With a great howl, it managed to break free, knocking her to the ground. It pounced on her, it pinned her to the ground and biting both her wings off. She screamed in agony, trying to push it away, but despite her best efforts it wouldn't budge.

She screamed for him to stop, that it was Lola, she loved him. But Leo didn't hear her. The beast engulfing him was overbearing, bent on destroying everything around him. It didn't care who this wretched thing was, only that it was in his way.

One last scream was heard, as her bones were crushed, her very being disappearing as her soul was destroyed. Without so much as a thread of emotion showing despite the heartbroken tear filled face left behind from her, it continued on its rampage. Leo truly had died turning into the beast this time, he had believed they killed Lola and was unable to bear the thought of losing her again. He had succumbed to his inner demon, this hell beast, letting it burn his very soul. He let it destroy his entire being to escape the pain, not knowing that it would be him who would ultimately kill her, his love.

Had she killed him, as she had been instructed to, at least this realm would have been safe. Now who could possibly stop him? Her soul was destroyed, forever lost to the expansive nothingness between existence and death. Could no one stop the beast now?

CH35: Mountain man.

There seemed to be nobody left to stop the beast as it crashed through nexus.

Lola, the one who could've destroyed the beast was now dead, and all hope seemed to be lost.

As it approached the next city, the residents of nexus took up their arms, a united front against this destructive devil. Upon its approach they could see the explosions on the horizon. Fear replaced by desperation, then clung tight to whatever they could find to use as weapons. Their efforts were vain, but the refused to give up without a fight. They had to at least try to stop it!

Slowly appearing on the horizon, towering over the distant sun, the beast began his assault. Fire pouring from its mouth, it charged into the city, leaving a trail of dark flames devouring the landscape behind it.

Parents stood in front of the children, a pathetic attempt to console there fear and protect them. At the charge of the beast, they let out a battery of cries, as they charged fourth toward certain death, weapons held high, determined to make some sort of difference.

Wasting no time the beast made quick work of them, but they refused to stop. Not even able to touch the beast, they remained undeterred. They continued the suicidal counter attack against the beast, trying to stop the end of this world.

Over all the carnage, explosions, and death, a sound was heard; A small boy crying, having just watched his mother die trying to shield him from the beast.

The beast was memorized by it, Frozen, as the boy continued to sob. The same broken hearted sob Leo had cried all those years ago, watching his family die. But this time there was no angel to save the boy, he would surely die.

Struggle broke out inside the beast, somewhere inside it, some fragment of Leo's being had somehow managed to survive; and was refusing to kill this child. He would not deprive him of a chance at life. He would not destroy it. It was just like Leo had been all those years ago. Without any other foreseeable savior Leo had managed to break back through, to save him.

The beast however didn't care, it only wanted to destroy. Born of anger, rage, grief, and sorrow, it knew only vengeance. Leo could barely even stop it from moving, and his fragmented soul was struggling just to accomplish that.

Just as it seemed all hope was lost, the beast was breaking free from the shred of humanity that had momentarily gripped it, something strange began to happen.

A giant wave of pressure shot out, as space started to distort, knocking the child away from the beast, just before it was crushed. A giant fist, made of earth formed from the ground, rising out, taking a humanoid form.

Born of a large mountain of earth, a giant stood before the beast. With a mighty wave of the hand it knocked the beast to the ground, quickly jumping to subdue it as quickly as possible. But, the beast was not done yet, ripping a huge chunk out of the throat of his attacker, causing the earth forming it to fall to the ground, causing it to lose all sense of form and collapse.

As it fell, another arm shot up from the ground, tripping the beast. And yet another arm formed from the earth, in a fist, striking the beast in the ribs.

No matter how many of these earthen forms the beast destroyed, more and more of them kept forming. It was an endless army of dirt.

The continuous onslaught of hits was greatly weighing down on the beast. Until, it finally got pinned down by these warriors of mud. A face formed in the earth, and shouted: "Grethhorsbane!" Two more hands formed around the beast, aiming directly at both of its heads.

In a giant distortion of space, and an ear splitting sonic boom, the flames began peeling from the beast while the earthen hands held it in place.

The howls it made while being torn apart almost loud enough to drown out all other sounds; except the sound of cheering. The citizens of nexus began celebrating, almost instantly, as the beast lay dying.

What was left of Leo, that had saved the child, was going to be forever lost as the remaining fragments of his corrupted soul disappeared into the abyss of nothingness left beyond death. With nothing to guide a soul back to another realm or plain, his soul simply ceases to exist. But, for him, this was merely retribution for the horrific actions he had committed.

As it dissolved into nothing, the small child, who had been saved by that small sliver of humanity left in the beast, was comforted by a hand on his shoulder;

And a voice speaking in a tone that could calm hell itself

"Don't be afraid to live your life young one."

Looking up to see who was speaking, he saw a man, aged from his experience, standing with an air of regret. The pain he had suffered through almost as obvious as his compassion for the boy. He stood up and walked away. Forever disappearing into the horizon, this was the last anybody ever saw of Leonardo Leon.

The boy's aunt ran up, gripping him tightly, and asked how he managed to survive what had appeared to be certain death.

"The man with the starry eyes saved me." The boy, never having known Leo or his name, could think of no other way to describe the man who had stood before him just a moment ago; who seemed so familiar.

She didn't understand, but she didn't care either, she was just glad he was alive.

"Let's go home Dante, your brother is worried about you."

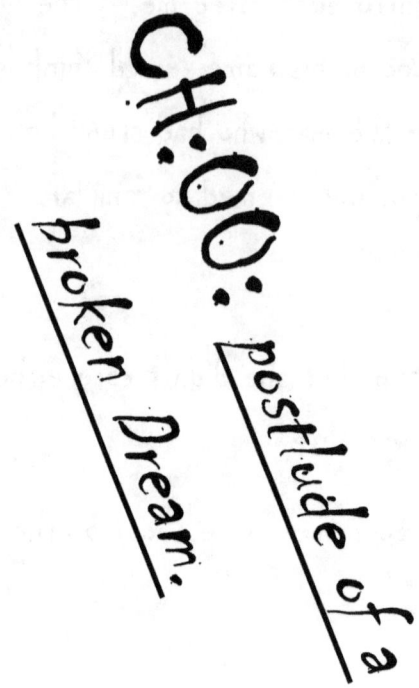

CH:00: postlude of a broken Dream.

As the death cycle continued, souls began to appear back in the ring realm. The abyss of destruction had been painstakingly rebuilt by John divine after he had managed to use the wall between realms to stop the beast from destroying nexus, he had used it like a suit of armor, protecting his soul from the beast and saving nexus. He was then able to expand the limbo between plains into the limbo between realms; ensuring chaos would never again fall on either realm.

"Sometimes all the world or the universe needs is a little divine intervention. When all hope is lost, you must never give up, just as your hope seems foolish, you too may one day see a divine intervention."

He had ascended from a mere mortal, through immortality, to the god of multiple realms. He was a truly just ruler. Everything he did, he did for the benefit of the souls in his realms. Passing on these the legends through generations, of the events that had happened, Of the Savior that was born from an insignificant soul, who changed his own fate. A story of Love that was lost.   It served as a warning of the corrosive effect that corruption, anger, fear, and revenge can have on a soul. They told of the power a soul can create when willed beyond its own limitations.

Throughout many hundreds of years that passed following the restoration of peace, the legend became shorter and shorter. Until, finally, one day it took on the form that has been passed down for so many generations that followed:

"It was a beast of a tale, the hero from hell, for love and revenge, his corruption his end. An angel of sky, once made him cry. With him the world cried; with him the world died. Leonardo Leon, one hell of a guy!"

END. :]

By:

Rob Thomas

www.ingramcontent.com/pod-product-compliance
Lightning Source LLC
Chambersburg PA
CBHW071254170626
46809CB00001B/220